She has also publised Warm Intrigues and
Traveling Streams with Trafford.

A GOLDEN LEAF

IN

REVISED

LYNN M. DIXON

Order this book online at www.trafford.com
or email orders@trafford.com

Most Trafford titles are also available at major online book retailers.

Printed in the United States of America.

ISBN: 978-1-4907-3072-1 (sc)
ISBN: 978-1-4907-3071-4 (e)

Trafford rev. 04/04/2014

 www.trafford.com

North America & international
toll-free: 1 888 232 4444 (USA & Canada)
fax: 812 355 4082

To my parents, Oscar and Hazel, to my sisters, and to all those who seek to triumph through life's storms.

Chapter 1

Phoenix's Faith

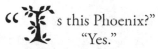 "**I**s this Phoenix?"

"Yes."

"Stay out of bed with my husband!" screamed the voice of the woman on the phone.

Phoenix listened calmly and said, "You must have the wrong person."

"No, I don't. This is Stan's wife, and I know that I am speaking to Phoenix Matthews. I am on my way to the library to let you know in person how I feel," said the woman before she slammed down the receiver. It was the wife of the part-time security guard at the library branch where Phoenix was a librarian.

Phoenix just sat there, speechless. Her two coworkers, who were listening to the conversation, just sat like stone lion statues at the oblong desk, privately joyous to see her discontent and humiliation.

"Problems?" Angelique, called Angel, grunted from one end of the circulation desk as she looked back down at the book she pretended to be reading to compete against Phoenix, whom she saw often reading. The other *statue* poured over a crossword puzzle and with no comment at all.

Before Phoenix came to the job as assistant library branch manager "from the north," Angel pretty much ran things at the library. The kids placated her by showering her with compliments, getting her lunch from neighborhood restaurants, or doing whatever they could to help her insecurity and need for constant attention for fear of her wrath. They privately knew that her wrath caused extreme pain, so they chose to pacify her and save themselves. They had witnessed her rage and hoped that it would not crop up again any time too soon.

Phoenix's arrival at the library caused Angel to feel threatened. She felt that her position as library assistant had lessened in importance and she was not going down without a fight. Angel was infuriated by the neighborhood children's love for Phoenix, so she constantly devised ways of making Phoenix's workdays a living hell.

Shortly after the phone call, a pregnant woman appeared at the door to the library. She had a bandanna tied around her head, and she had two small children with her. She took one look at Phoenix and shouted in front of the morning senior-citizen patrons, "Stay out of bed with my husband, or I'll hurt you!"

Phoenix stood there in a pink two-piece cotton suit with her mouth agape. She felt the blood rush to her head and felt a light dizziness, not knowing what to do.

The branch manager hurried out of his office. He took one look at Phoenix and quickly suggested that Phoenix, the security guard-husband, and the wife and children come into his office to deter further outbursts and embarrassment. As they moved into the small office, it felt airless. There was only room for two persons to be seated. The branch manager sat behind his desk, and Phoenix sat on a high stool. The security guard and the wife stood along the wall.

The children cried out of confusion. The wife accused. The branch manager attempted to mediate. The security guard stood and studied the rug. Phoenix studied the city map on the wall, never realizing that the city had so many streets. The wife talked on and on. The air thickened in the unventilated office, and what was all of twenty minutes seemed like an eternity.

The door of the small office finally opened. Of course, there was no resolution. So from the office emerged a mummy-like Phoenix, a pained and embarrassed security guard, an outraged wife with two confused children, and a branch manager with a distant look in his eyes.

At the desk sat the two statues who never looked up and who were secretly grinning after seeing Phoenix caught off guard. Phoenix, tearful yet too immobilized to cry, simply went to her desk and retrieved a small book from her purse. She walked to the ladies room and shut the door and made sure it was locked. She sat for a moment in disbelief before opening her *Daily Word* magazine. She read a few lines and tried to calm down and get centered enough to complete the workday.

She emerged from the ladies room walking with a level of composure. She avoided contact with others and found quiet work to focus on until the workday ended. Whenever the anxiety returned, she repeated a reassuring line from Og Mandino's *The Greatest Salesman in the World*. Inaudibly, she said "I will persist until I succeed" until she felt calm again.

After that particular workday, the wife of the security guard decided that she would come to work with her husband regularly to watch. She insisted that it was a public place and that she had rights. On Fridays, when it was time for Phoenix to show movies to the neighborhood children, it was the security guard's duty to keep the kids in line. The wife would be there in the darkroom to make sure there was nothing going on. Phoenix merely could not understand where the wife had gotten the notion that there was any reason for concern, but after looking over at Angel's smug attitude, she had a pretty good idea who had planted the seed.

The library was in an old district of the city which needed all the self-love and dignity that it could muster. It was in a low-income area with a public housing unit situated behind it and close to a landfill. There were plenty of unwed teenage mothers, broken homes, and an overabundance of little children, all living on the fringes of society.

The library served as their oasis in a mound of problems, and Phoenix and the branch manager had larger visions. They knew the importance of providing a reprieve from life's storms to the troubled community. The provision of books, puppet shows, story hours, and constant school and day-care visits were high priorities to those who could see the big picture.

He and Phoenix had developed a two-year strategic plan. They were going to experiment with various techniques to upgrade circulation by increasing the collection, promoting reading to all ages and purchasing educational toys for the children. They had already increased the visits to the local middle schools, elementary schools, and day care centers.

Phoenix attempted to answer some of those needs by ordering, and reading from, books with positive images for the children of color. But everyone did not see the big picture because they were blinded by their egos and personal needs.

Upon entering the library, one felt like exhaling. There were beautiful hanging plants and two very large aquariums. The sound of the moving water in the fish tanks added to the welcoming ambience the library extended to its guests. This was a place of refuge for many who needed to experience the sense of peace that it offered.

The library was attached to a community health clinic, and if a person was driving past, they would just see two adjoining cement buildings in an impoverished neighborhood. It was either one had to enter to feel the warmth at the door of the library, or they would know to enter from prior visits or word of mouth.

This community was rich in culture, and the housing development was filled with wide-eyed, precious children who looked forward to running into the library for its regular programs. On the good days when Phoenix felt attuned to her mission, she enjoyed the children's laughter and their enthusiasm as she read them stories and exposed them to the beauty of books. She enjoyed watching the very young preschoolers touch their first books and flip through the pages, knowing that it could be their passage out of the land of the desolate.

These reflective thoughts surfaced as Phoenix left work that day. She was shaken but still standing. When she reached her car in the library parking lot, she noticed that the car emblem on the Mercury had been broken off. She paused, took a deep breath, and got in her car. She listened to the love songs playing on the car radio and headed home, trying to tune out the events of the day.

As she drove from the library, she could see the broken glass, broken windows, and boarded-up businesses, all representatives of broken dreams. As she got closer and closer to the university area, the streets widened, the houses became neater and more prosperous, and the shrubbery became more beautiful. *Such is life,* she thought. *The haves and the have-nots. Low self-esteems and high self-esteems. The dichotomy of life. But,* she thought, *you can only help those who will receive it.*

While stopping at one intersection, Phoenix felt guided to look up. She witnessed a beautiful loop of the clouds in the sky. She received the quick but sturdy message that this was God's brushstroke of artistry reminding her that he had a shield of protection around her. Comforted, she forged ahead feeling a little lighter. She pulled into the parking lot at her apartment complex.

The university, situated close by, was a lifeline for her. Even if not actively involved on the campus, she could still go over and listen to speakers, or watch bands practice or whatever was going on to remind herself that she was still part of a vibrant world. The university was like a breath of fresh air, and it helped sustain her.

She trudged up the steps to her apartment feeling somewhat weighted down by the events of the day. She thought, *It is entirely too much!* She plopped down on her short white love seat. First, she just sat and stared into space for a while. Finally, she changed into jeans and a T-shirt. She went to the refrigerator and reached for a can of beer. She wasn't the best cook, and it was getting to the point that the kitchen was basically being used to house "these friends." She assured herself that she was just trying to relax.

Deep within, she knew, above all other things, that this *relaxing* was getting out of hand. *Just try to stop thinking. Just stop thinking. Stop replaying the tape.*

Phoenix had come south to attend a historically black university and had successfully graduated with a second degree. She had begun to enjoy the great climate and the slower pace. She chose to move a tad further north to the mid-south where she had a family base. She thoroughly enjoyed the laughter with visiting cousins, the fish fries, and the outings to concerts and clubs.

The southern cooking was also a big hook, and she liked eating the scrumptious meals and attending the numerous cookouts, but now she had begun to feel restlessness and felt that change was in the winds. Perhaps she was outgrowing this scene. Phoenix knew that her confidence and strength were waning, and her discontent was growing.

Later that evening, Phoenix listened to some smooth jazz and hoped that she could muster the strength to return to the "war zone." She leaned over, reached for her Bible, and flipped to the ever-comforting book of Psalms. She found a passage in the Bible saying, "His leaf shall not wither and whatsoever he doeth shall prosper" (Psalm 1:3). Phoenix took some consolation in that verse and prayed that she would not wither before fulfilling her mission. Sleepily, she admitted that things seemed to be unmanageable but knew that her faith would get her through to higher ground.

She fluffed her pillow in its royal-blue silk pillowcase and propped it under her head and tried to relax. She made sure that the alarm clock was set to get her up through the fog enveloping her mind. She fell asleep vowing, "I'll be stronger and better in the morning." In regard to her own ensuing problems, she promised to turn over a new leaf.

Chapter 2

Trey's Faith

As the alarm clock went off, he whispered, "Oh, God, help me. I feel as though I just lay down, and I have to fly with *that* man today. I'm so tired." He sighed as he thought about the late night before. "Got to stop doing this," he chuckled. Trey lazily sat up and rubbed his eyes as he thought about the flight to Atlanta. He had to be a facilitator at a literary conference. The thought motivated him to get up and start his day.

Trey got out of bed slowly, showered, dried, and began to dress. He chose a dark-blue thin-pinstriped suit that he felt was perfect for his role as speaker. As he buttoned his light-blue shirt, Trey decided on a royal-blue tie. Just as he had completed the last knot, the phone began to ring. It seemed to be ringing three times faster than usual. All he could think of was "Desperado."

"Hello?" questioned Trey.

"Hi. It's me. Did you enjoy last night?" she asked. "I just called to say have a great trip. Will you call me when you get there?"

"Well, uh—" started Trey.

"How come you didn't ask me to take you to the airport?" Flora cut in.

"I, uh—" he began.

"Is it okay if I fly down on Saturday after your conference? I have not seen Atlanta. I have heard of Underground Atlanta and the Coca-Cola museum and we can—" she started.

"Flora!" he cut in. "Please let me call you when I get there. I'm running late. I have a flight to catch, and I'm running late," he said emphatically.

"But I just wanted us to be together and—" she continued.

"Flora, please," he stated firmly but softly.

"Okay," she whimpered like a hurt puppy. "If you don't want to be bothered, all you had to do was say so."

"Flora, I'll call you when I get to Atlanta."

"Okay." She lingered, allowing the intended guilt to fill the spaces.

"Good-bye," he said and hung up the phone. *Gosh,* he thought. *If she would give me breathing space, I could think of some things we both could enjoy other than good food, music, and sex. She doesn't give me a chance to think!* his thoughts screamed.

When he thought of Flora, he thought of how comfortable he used to feel when he was at her place. He could smell the spices from her great cooking. Good aromas always seemed to pour from the kitchen. In fact, everything smelled good to him—then. As the old saying goes, "Sugar and spice and everything nice." But that was then. Now *discomfort* seemed to be the going word.

How can she be so incredibly insecure? She always thinks I am with someone else. She doesn't understand the concentration required doing my work, and she always has an alternate plan working outside of mine without first consulting me. She always has one up. *Does she ever sleep?* he wondered as he slammed his luggage closed. He was thrown somewhat off balance by these bombarding thoughts.

A cantankerous Trey grumbled down the porch steps. The thoughts swirled as he continued toward his car. *I put down my writing when she called last night and went on over there after she made me feel guilty. Now I'm not quite prepared but I will get it together once I reach the Atlanta hotel,* his thoughts continued.

Maybe if Flora read some books or had some interests of her own, we could better relate. She only reads what I'm reading to stay plugged into my mind like a socket, and I resent that! I feel like she siphons my energy like a vampire.

Trey knew deep within himself that he had chosen her for all the wrong reasons. When they first met, she fed his ego, gave in to his every whim, and challenged nothing. He had taken the path of least resistance, but now—now things were different. She was becoming an agitation to his soul.

It had been three years. Her job as an administrative assistant with the city ended with the workday. She obviously had no interest in advancing herself, so her free time conflicted with his job that required large amounts of home study. Her church life didn't seem to require any home study either. Her only requirement in life was to report, and after work, her life became a pursuit of *him*.

After getting in the car with a huff, he slammed the door, turned the ignition, and searched for some soothing music on the car radio. He only got jumpy, loud DJs screaming about waking up and cracking silly jokes. After some searching, he found a calming, hopeful voice— Stevie Wonder singing "Ribbon in the Sky."

He envisioned meeting his dream woman as an anecdote to his real and present angst. He had heard from his grandfather in his early years that daydreaming was not masculine, but at this stage in his life, he held tightly to his dreams because the reality of his love life was too hard to bear. Dreams were all he had! For a moment, he felt reassured that better days lay ahead.

Trey tried to push the clingy Flora from his mind, and the music helped him ease through traffic as he headed toward O'Hare Airport. Once he reached the airport, he affirmed *divine order* and found a parking space in the long-term parking lot.

When he arrived at the ticket counter, there stood the grinning, conniving Hank, who was privately envious of Trey's talent and integrity. He called out, "Hey there. Thought you wouldn't make it. Looks like you had a rough night. Straighten up your tie! Do you have your ticket?"

Trey just answered "Yes" to all these negative digs and started walking toward the airplane gate. He thought, *Slugs*—as one author called them. "Lord, give me strength," Trey said under his breath.

Once Trey and Hank were seated on the 737, Hank started up as though someone had put a quarter in him. During the flight, he never took a breather. He started about his life from when he was twelve and had only reached the sixteenth year by the time the flight landed in Atlanta. The only relief that Trey found was looking out of the window and imagining that the drone of Hank's voice was just the hum of the airplane engine.

Damn, thought Trey. *If only he would just hush!* But no such luck.

Once they landed, Trey had the new experience of riding the computer-operated subway. He found it a bit eerie—like the headless horseman—once he saw that there was no driver. But due to the immensity of the airport, he had no choice but to get with the flow. *Wow,* he thought. *Can't imagine the Chicago EL without a driver.* "Technology!" he breathed.

They caught a shuttle to the downtown hotel where the conference was being held. As they headed north from the airport, Trey noticed the tall, legendary Georgia pine trees and the vast spaciousness of the hot Georgian landscape while still on the outskirts of town.

As they neared the inner city, he noticed the bottlenecked traffic, and he was glad that he was not driving. He remembered reading that Atlanta was landlocked, and the thick, muggy weather proved it to be true as the perspiration gathered around his neck. He loosened his tie to breathe more easily.

Once they arrived at the hotel, he checked in, received his key, and took the elevator up to his room. He opened the door to his room, closed the door, and felt a surge of peace enveloping him. He came out of the now hot suit, stripped down to his underwear, slumped down in one of the easy chairs, and sought to just relax from it all.

After what seemed like hours, he slowly picked up his literary reviews and research and started cleaning up a few blotches. The ideas of his upcoming literary presentation all came back with great clarity as he worked on his findings. He smiled. *Boy, my mind was certainly moving last night before Flora called. I was really on a roll,* he thought as he continued to edit his work.

After about an hour and a half of intense work, Trey, finally satisfied with the correcting process, rose and decided to shower. Once in the shower, he showered slowly and intensely. He dried off and splashed on some cologne. He began to smile slightly as his mind seemed to smoothen out a bit.

At that moment, the Atlanta sunshine came through the window at an angle and fell on his manuscript. Rainbows seemed to emanate from the water glass onto the paper. *Good omen.* He smiled. The phone rang at that instant. *Probably Hank saying he's ready to go to the first session,* he thought.

"Hello?" answered Trey.

"Hi, honey. I just wanted to see if you made it okay. How was it? You said that you would call when you got there," Flora quizzed.

Before he could fully answer her, there was a knock at the door. "Hold on, Flora," Trey stressed. "Let me see who's knocking." He put down the phone and went to the hotel door.

"Okay, man," he said to Hank. "I'll be down."

When he picked the phone back up, he heard, "Whose Mamie?" Flora's voice rose.

"Flora, that was Hank. I said *man*, not *Mamie!*" he boomed.

"Yeah, right. Is that why you did not want me to come? Is it your old girlfriend you never got over in the south? I should have known!" she screamed. Then she started to cry and whimper like a hurt child.

As the accusations burst forth like water from a broken dam, she cried and cried. Trey's soul cried and cried. When he could find his voice, he hoarsely said, "Flora, I'll call you tonight at nine after the last speech. Okay?"

No answer.

"Okay?" he continued. "Now calm down. Calm down."

"Okay," she cooed, knowing that she now had his attention, regardless of the means.

As he hung up the phone, he felt the steam lift from his head. *Lord, give me strength and faith that this will work out somehow. I am sorry. So sorry I touched her. Sorry I was weak for her and so sorry I accepted the gifts. Sorry I accepted the gold chain for Christmas. Sorry I spoke to her. Sorry, sorry, sorry! Sorry I ate her food. Oh, Lord, help me,* he thought. His spirit broken and enthusiasm waning, he searched his mind to think of a line that would help him at a time like this. Finally, he came up with a line from Og Mandino's *The Greatest Salesman in the World*. "I will master my emotions."

When he thought of how hard he had worked on his presentation, he knew he'd better snap out of the blue phase. He started to dress, and as he put on each piece of clothing, he vaguely admitted that his life was becoming a bit unmanageable. This mate was beginning to affect his ability to do his job well.

He took a few moments and closed his eyes in prayer. He opened the hotel Bible placed by the Gideons, and it opened to 1 Peter 3. His eyes seemed to fall on the eighth verse when it spoke of husbands and wives. He knew that he wanted a wife with whom he could "Be ye all of one mind, having compassion one of another, love as brethren, be pitiful, be courteous."

He knew that this woman could *not* be Flora, who had so little consideration for his nor her own emotional balance. Again, he chose his royal-blue tie to hold on to his shaken faith that things would be okay. He looked out of the window and up at the beautiful magenta-and-blue sky for the faith and strength to see this professional endeavor through with clarity. He sat for a few minutes, breathed deeply, and rose to go down and meet Hank for the opening of the conference with a slight sorrow in his heart.

Chapter 3
Phoenix's Strength

Phoenix awakened with the thought, *Well, I am not sorry. I will not go around apologizing for my presence.* She pouted. Then she pressed down hard on the pillow to keep the disturbing thoughts from surfacing. *It's not my fault that Angel was allowed to grow up as a weed that goes around trying to destroy others.*

At that moment, Phoenix clicked on the light because her mind wouldn't let her rest. She turned off the music, which only calmed her for a while. She saw that it was 4:00 a.m., and she had to be back there at 10:00 a.m. "Just a few hours left to rest. A few hours left to rest," she repeated. She sat up in her bed, reached over to her nightstand, and picked up her ever-present legal pad. Scribbling on a sheet of paper, "Pensive thoughts . . . pensive thoughts . . ." That was as far as she got because there were few pensive thoughts at the moment. She stopped writing and let the moment have its way.

Thoughts, not so pensive, came bursting forth. She thought of one of her few safety nets and place of refuge in this lonely town being currently invaded, her closest friend. Then it all came to the center of her brain like a stream overflowing. Him. "His house was one of the few places I could go and feel a sense of safety. It wasn't perfect, but it was special," she murmured to herself.

She thought of the comfortable house with the host who always greeted her with a cheery "Come on in the house." He always made sure she was fed for he liked to cook. His meals were tasty and well seasoned, and she liked watching his mastery in the kitchen. The smells from the open kitchen and the smell of him and his balmy surroundings gave her a feeling of warmth that she missed.

It was not a neat lifestyle, but a relaxed one. Papers were strewn everywhere, which she helped to arrange when allowed. It looked like the house of a mad scientist because it was the house of a man who thought and pondered things deeply.

She recalled the good times like the day she sat on the steps orally rehearsing her French as he planted trees in the backyard. At that time, she could not see how they could ever become full-grown trees. But she took his word for it since he had planted the huge poplar tree in the front yard. And as promised, she witnessed those in the backyard becoming baby trees too.

She realized that they were proof of the longevity of their journey together. That's why she'd found this intrusion at such a delicate time extremely hard. But intrusions are never well-timed, though often inevitable.

Deep within, she knew that the relationship was not completely fulfilling, and there were no prospects for the future. But this was all too hard to face at once. But now she suspected him spending time with her close friend whom she had told so much. "Guess I shared too much about him," she spoke audibly. She started to repeat to herself, "I can't think about that. Can't. Cannot."

Again she started writing, "Pensive thoughts, pensive moods, ease the friction of the mind. Restores the strength for pre-made goals; destinations not fantasized, but attainable. 'Reaches' that bring back the bounce of existence. And vigor, fight, and aggressiveness akin to survival." She stopped, paused. She hoped that the positives that she had written would reach deep into her soul.

Feeling a bit better, Phoenix lay back down and fell into a deep sleep. It seemed as though she had been asleep for hours when she woke up wringing wet. She had just dreamt of the awful pain of seeing her best friend with her lover in crystal-clear vision. After trying to calm down, realizing that it might be better for the pain to surface, Phoenix just lay still saying, "I'll overcome this one too. I have the strength," she assured herself. A few hours later, after some restless sleep, she crawled out of bed with a heavy head, a burdened heart, and a cloudy mind. She thought that perhaps she felt depleted because she was using her spiritual and mental substance in the wrong places.

Beginning to know that this type of existence was taking its toll on her, Phoenix quietly asked for strength so that she could cope with another day at the office. She found a line or two from a Ponder book to reassure her that all was well.

The alarm clock sounded. She looked up at her high oblong window where the birds chose to build a nest. Their chirping always let her know that day was breaking. Their music was like a friendly serenade saying it's time to get up. She laid there for a while and just listened. She rose out of bed, went to the bathroom, and dazedly grabbed a facecloth. She washed her face, cried some, got herself a glass of water, and lay back down and further rested.

She rose and began to prepare for her workday, knowing deep within that she was in no state to report. She was still too emotional and sleep-deprived to face those who strove to destroy her.

Bombarded by her job crisis and her failing romance, she felt exasperated. She deeply longed for a touch, a listening ear, a heartfelt pat on the shoulder, or anything to let her know that she was not carrying all of this alone. But her faith reminded her that there were invisible forces and helpers all along the way.

But then she remembered the words of Eddy, who said, "There is a cross to be taken up before we can enjoy the fruition of our hope and faith." She showered, dressed in a dark-green linen suit, and forged ahead to report, bearing her cross and all.

Chapter 4
Trey's Strength

Trey entered his hotel room late in the evening after the third day of the literary conference. First, he removed his suit coat. His presentation as one of panel speakers had gone well. He had received many compliments afterward. Some of the questions were rather thought-provoking during the Q and A, but he had handled it well and was glad that he had sufficiently studied.

He took off his tie and unbuttoned his shirt. After sitting down in a chair by the window, he removed his tight-fitting dress shoes and breathed. He simply sat in silence and started to unwind as he lazily took in the sights and sounds of Atlanta. He noted the movement of the people down on the ever-bustling Peachtree Street.

"Free at last!" he sighed. He got up and poured himself a glass of wine from the hotel refrigerator. He sipped it slowly as he reflected on the days. They liked his theories on spirituality in early American literature. He realized how much energy he had exerted in speaking, traveling, and in preparation. He exhaled heavily.

Just as Trey closed his eyes and started to relax, the phone rang. He thought, *It's probably Flora. Lord, what am I going to do with this woman? She doesn't give me a chance to breathe.* He had been talking with her every day after the conference sessions. So on this evening, he chose to not to answer the phone. He needed a moment.

The phone rang and rang. He sat there and looked at it and wondered when it would stop. Finally, the ringing stopped, and there was the blinking light that he felt held him captive. He tried to ignore the flashing, but it was hard to do so. In about fifteen minutes, the ringing started again. It went on and on. Surely the person on duty at the front desk felt as sorry for being at work as Trey felt for ever having touched this woman!

He sat quietly now. His enthusiasm waned quickly as he transformed into a stone-like sculpture. He felt like a shell of a man because he felt helpless in knowing how to handle this situation.

Trey remembered when he had first met Flora and how she had been a great comfort because he had recently lost his mother. He was very close to his mother, and he could talk with her about a lot of things. Flora had been an emotional anchor when he felt that his world was falling apart. She kept good meals around and would let him mosey around her place and not pry into his thoughts. She was often quiet, which he mistook for being peaceful.

But now it seemed that the stronger he became emotionally, the more insecure she seemed to become. She was driving them apart with her accusations and was becoming more of a burden to their relationship. Perhaps he had misread some signs somewhere down the line. He just hadn't quite figured it out.

He had tried to reassure her and make her feel more secure, but nothing seemed to work. She talked of marriage often, and he felt uncomfortable with the idea because she had not met him halfway. Nothing he liked seemed to interest her, such as going to games or playing board games or listening to various genres of music. She leaned toward the reality shows and fashion. He had often seen her cutting out pictures of brides. He was not against the idea of marriage but he wanted to be in a healthy relationship and his doubts were surmounting.

He realized that the phone had finally stopped ringing. He slept lightly for a while and immediately felt guilty. *Oh well,* he thought as he walked over to the phone. "I can't get any peace anyway," he found himself saying aloud. He rang Flora's number, and the phone rang six or seven times. As he was about to hang up, she picked up lazily and said very weakly, "Hello."

"Flora, it's Trey!"

"It's eleven at night there," she slurred.

"What's wrong with your voice, Flora?" Trey asked.

"I, I, I—" she mumbled.

"I *what?*" His voice rose.

"I took some sleeping pills. You said that you were going to call at nine. I felt that you had probably met someone else, and I just didn't want to think about it anymore," she dragged. She sounded drugged, and he began to lose control. He called her name.

No answer.

"Flora!" he said, louder.

No answer.

"Flora? Flora!" he said, much louder.

He heard the phone drop. He started shaking like a leaf and he kept hollering into the phone, "Flora!"

Still no answer.

He started to get dressed as he searched for Flora's sister's number. He called her sister and told her to hurry and get over there because she had keys to Flora's place. He told her that he would catch the next flight home.

Before leaving the hotel, he went by Hank's and told him that he had to quit the conference because of a "family emergency." He purposely left out the details because he knew that Hank was far from being a trusted friend.

After Trey had left his room, Hank just sat back with his huge belly, which barely allowed him to relax in the small hotel chair. *Yeah,* he thought, *you folks always got some kind of 'family emergency.' Probably just wanted to get back to that gal of his.* He snickered. He had assured Trey that he would take care of everything—and that he would definitely do.

Trey called his father back long distance and imparted the story. Elisha listened and said, "Calm down, son. Pick up Fillmore's *The Twelve Powers of Man* that I gave you, and read the chapter on 'Love' on your flight. Try to hold her in a high light and pray for her to either fall into understanding or quietly move on out of your life. Call me when you get to Chicago."

He threw his clothes in the luggage, unfolded. He stacked all his conference papers and shoved them into his briefcase. He carefully checked around the room to make sure that he had all his possessions. He hurried down to the checkout desk and let them know he was departing early and was willing to pay for any penalties if necessary.

He was able to book a flight, and he boarded the airport shuttle and headed for the Hartsfield-Jackson Atlanta Airport.

Once the shuttle arrived at the airport, he went inside the terminal. He saw that he still had an hour before boarding, so he found the first bar and ordered a double scotch on the rocks. He checked his watch, headed toward the gate with a buzzing head, and tried to even his breathing. He resolved to use his mental and spiritual might to face what lay ahead. He wiped his sweating brow with a green napkin from the bar and went to board the plane headed to Chicago.

Chapter 5

Phoenix's Wisdom

As Phoenix drove to work, her thoughts raced a million miles a minute for her day in the office. She tried to make herself feel better and repeated, "I am a miracle on course." However, on this day, she was not convinced. As she got closer and closer to the library, her knees started shaking, and she felt ill.

About four blocks before reaching the library, she pulled over to the side of the street and gave her stomach a chance to settle. She knew that she had not been eating properly She sat awhile and tuned into a spiritual station as she attempted regain some composure. Almost as if on autopilot, she turned the car around in the opposite direction.

I just can't handle it today, she thought. *Not today.* She gripped both hands tightly around the steering wheel. She went directly to a house where she knew she'd be welcomed.

She slowed down as she approached the house on Foster. She was reluctant to interrupt her aunt and uncle's morning routines with her problems. Her uncle was retired, and her aunt didn't work outside the home. But after pausing, she pulled into the long driveway which led to the house on the hill. She knew they'd heard the car engine, so she completed the incline and turned off the engine.

She went up the stairs listening to the wind blowing through the beautiful and decorative wind chimes that her aunt kept on the front porch. Her aunt's green thumb was evident through all the beautiful plants seated all around the porch, which helped to roll out the welcome mat to all the visitors.

She rang the bell lightly. Her uncle came to the door, and when he saw her state, he helped her inside. She began to cry uncontrollably, and after she reassured him that no one had died, she asked him to call her supervisor and tell him that she would not be in that day. "I just can't go in there today," she said over and over as she shook her head.

Her aunt, her mother's younger sister, told her to calm down, and after they talked awhile, she went to shower. Her aunt gave her some loungewear to change into for the rest of day. Later, after having breakfast, they sat out in the greenhouse and continued to relax and talk. Her aunt shared the beauty of patience as she nurtured her beloved flowers as they grew.

She had an abundance of crape myrtles, which she explained came from the Natchez area. She talked about her dogwood flowers, which had to be cut back to avoid them from growing into trees. She pointed to her honeysuckle plants and told Phoenix that they grow easily. She said that she often cut off some pieces and put them in water to give the house a pleasant aroma. And lastly, she talked about her special rose bushes. She was especially proud of her sweetheart roses, which she spent time cutting back as they relaxed in the backyard.

This was a great way for Phoenix to forget her own issues and learn the great lessons of patience that she was being taught as her aunt talked about her plants. She saw that all works of beauty and art took time to develop and grow. They later went inside, and she was further comforted by having a hearty long-distance conversation with her mother, Septima.

She poured out her heart and emptied the "toxins" from her system. Her mother's closing words were, "Remember, Phoenix, that no person, no thing, no set of circumstances can by any possibility interpose itself between you and your good. They are there for your own spiritual growth. I know you can't see it now, but you will. They're like growing pains. Your higher good is on the way. Something good will come behind this. Try to relax, and try not thinking about it for today anyway. Enjoy your stay there and your day off."

Earlier, she overheard her uncle talking to her supervisor, saying angrily, "I don't know what is going in that library, but my niece will *not* be in today." He was known for his gruffness, and Phoenix was certain that her young boss felt the pain.

Phoenix looked around the guest room of her aunt and uncle's home where she had been coming for many years of her life. The bright colors of the curtains, matching bedspread, and the familiar walnut furniture helped her relax. She dozed as she smelled the onions and green peppers coming from the kitchen. *Something good is cooking.* She smiled.

Phoenix slept awhile but was awakened with an unsettling feeling. She faced her pain as she saw the smiling face of her friend Lila. The smile was not a happy one but more of a sneer. She opened her eyes and remembered that she was at her aunt's house. She rolled over and pulled the covers up as if this would shield her from some disturbing information that was trying to seep into her mind. There stood the truth—Lila and her friend. "Could this really be going on? Are they both really that tricky?" she asked herself.

That spring day that she and Lila had traveled to a coworker's mother's funeral in Mississippi all came back to her. She had driven, and Lila agreed to accompany her. She was glad to have the company because it was a trip she needed to make and not one that she wanted to make alone in the Mississippi backwoods.

The trip took about two hours each way, and it was like taking a trip back down a time capsule. The red dirt of the road was on both sides of the highway. The houses were old and often had peeling paint. There were several trailer homes along the way, which were common in those parts because they were probably more affordable.

After they finally reached the small country town, they found the church after asking for directions. People always stared when they saw city people, and they saw the Tennessee tags and knew that she and Lila were not from those surrounding parts.

The funeral was long. The minister did his best, but to Phoenix, his sermon was so dark because it made everyone feel guilty for being alive. She was so glad for the positive-thinking path that she had embarked upon. Anyway, they got through the funeral and even went to the cemetery as they saw the whole ordeal through to completion.

Phoenix and Lila exhaled as they entered the highway taking them back farther north. Phoenix never thought the Tennessee state line sign could look so inviting. She and Lila breathed out as they crossed it.

They both laughed. She told Lila that before she took her home, she was going to stop by her friend's house to let him know that she was back. He lived close to the state line.

"Okay." Lila smiled.

When she pulled into his driveway and tooted the horn, he came out. He leaned in on Phoenix's side and told her that he was glad that they had had a safe trip. She turned and introduced him to Lila, but before she could finish the formal introduction, Lila got out of the car and went around to where he was standing, touched him on his arm, and said, "Ooh. Let me touch you and see if you are for real. I have heard so much about you, and now I know that you exist," cooed Lila.

He just pulled back slightly, a little bit embarrassed but quite flattered. Before Lila came to her senses, she handed him one of her business cards. Phoenix was shocked as she drove Lila home. There were no words. She couldn't believe what the presence of a man brought out in some women.

It seemed as if things changed between her and Lila. Lila was more distant and less available, and when Phoenix was in Lila's company, she was more critical and curt. Her behavior bordered on straight hostility, and their relationship became more strained. She was led to back off until she could see what was really going on.

Phoenix sat up in her aunt's bed, pulling her knees up toward her as she started to feel queasy inside. She knew that she would hold steady and be guided to make good decisions regarding her dilemmas. When she felt that things were never going to happen, she enjoyed reading the reassuring lines of Burroughs's poem, "Waiting." She calmed herself, realizing that no one could take what was rightfully hers. So she concluded by saying, "Evidently, this man is not mine." She picked up her work briefcase for some writing paper. She took out a pen and was inspired to write a poem. She titled it "Library Loans," and it read,

> *Lord, give me no more library loans.*
> *I'm tired of borrowing.*
> *Though the usage is divine,*
> *The returning leaves me in a pine.*
> *I'm ready for mine. I feel it's truly time!*

Once she completed the poem, she put her latest creation in her case and pulled the yellow comforter closer up around her neck. She felt that she should go to church on Sunday in an effort to search for the right path. She dozed off, and pleasant dreams came right away as she vowed to continue to turn over a new leaf.

Chapter 6
Trey's Wisdom

Once aboard the flight, Trey took his seat, took deep breaths and anticipated his flight home. He flipped open the *Atlanta Constitution* newspaper that he had bought in the airport. He scanned the headlines nervously, attempting to read though his thoughts were jumping all over the place. Nothing was soaking in, so he folded it and put it away. He turned to his new *Atlanta Magazine*. He didn't want to appear as a low-level reader, but at least the great colors of the photography held his attention. It helped him appear to be a calm business traveler as he anxiously waited to see what was going on with Flora.

Just as he settled back into his seat, he heard someone say in a booming voice, "Trey? Man, is that you?" He turned around and saw his old college roommate. He was seated in the next aisle across from him. He had shared rooms with him during his freshman year in college.

"Hey, Bill. How are you?" Trey asked.

"How've you been, Trey?" asked Bill.

"Okay, man. Okay," responded Trey.

"What type of work are you doing?"

"I'm a professor of literature," answered Trey.

"Oh, that's great! I am presently an accountant with one of the Fortune 500 companies." Bill smiled.

Trey turned to get a better glimpse of Bill. He noticed the carefully manicured nails, the large diamond ring, the diamond earring stud in one ear, and the extremely thin nylon socks that Bill wore. He noticed how he was giving undivided attention to himself and kept patting his hair in place.

Hmm, thought Trey.

Just then, they were alerted to fasten their seatbelts for takeoff. As the plane increased its velocity, Trey leaned back and closed his eyes. As he did so, memories of the unwelcome past soared as the plane heightened. *Damn,* he thought. *When it rains it pours.*

A smooth takeoff brought a sigh of relief from Trey and also brought the flight attendant.

"Sir? Sir? Can I get you anything?"

"*Yes,*" Trey answered emphatically. "A glass of white wine, please."

"Okay, sure," she said understandingly.

Trey sipped the wine slowly as he tried to suppress the memory of the night he woke up in his dorm room—the night Bill made advances toward him, and he was totally caught off guard. He now knew that he had not handled the situation well, but no one had prepared him for this type of encounter.

Trey had jumped up and hit Bill in the face, and Bill had whimpered like a hurt child, blood dripping from his upper left brow.

"Man, what is wrong with you?" hollered Trey. "I am sorry, but you should know that I don't roll like that. What were you thinking?" Trey's voice trembled.

Trey immediately put on a shirt and some jeans and headed out of the dorm. Thankfully, he was able to visit the girl he was dating, who had an apartment off campus. She took one look at him and just let him in and never asked questions. He now reflected again on how he had let a perceptive gem slip through his fingers when he had let her get away.

The next day, after trudging through his final exams, Trey raced to the Greyhound station and headed home. He felt queasy and uneasy and was determined to find an apartment off campus when he returned for the next semester. He did.

He looked over at Bill now and felt a sense that this was another thing cropping up from his past that needed attention. He got up when it was safe to do so and went over to Bill. He cleared his throat and said, "Hey look, man, I am sorry for that night." He felt that it was the wise thing to say.

Bill responded, "It's all right, Trey. I read some things wrong. I want you to forgive me also. I was going through a rough patch after losing my dad."

It's all good, man," Trey closed, and they shook hands.

Bill gave Trey one of his business cards and said, "If you ever need some help with some numbers, contact me."

"Thanks," said Trey. "You never know." He put the card in his wallet. "I am a word person, but who knows. I may hit it big one day and need someone with keen financial advice to help me."

Trey went on to the lavatory while he was up, and when the door was locked, he sat there for a minute. The anxious thoughts seemed to subside, and a feeling of calm surrounded him. He intuitively felt that this wrong had been righted. He washed his hands and returned to his seat. He and Bill acknowledged one another with light smiles. It gave him the confidence to go forward and handle the situation that awaited him.

He finally dozed off a little, and his thoughts made him face the fact that he had contributed to Flora's current state. Perhaps he had been too busy or too wound up in his own work to see that she was capable of hurting herself. He had been enjoying all the amenities and benefits and did not truly take the time to check on her mental state. Now he realized that he might not even be able to give her what she felt she needed.

The captain's voice came on the speaker announcing that they should prepare for landing. Once the plane was safely on the ground, the passengers began to deplane. He waved at Bill, and after getting his luggage, he walked out to where he bypassed the yellow cabs and boarded a shuttle to the long-term parking area. He could now release the old pains of the past, and he hoped that he would be guided as he faced the uncertain present scene.

Chapter 7

Phoenix's Love

Sunday morning arrived, and Phoenix was at home again after a restful day with her aunt and uncle. She awakened to the cool breeze of the mid-southern air and the chattering birds that had built a nest beside her air-conditioner. She was glad to be on her own turf and she got up and fixed a pot of coffee.

While it was brewing, she decided to go to one of the local churches that she'd heard so much about. She drank her coffee slowly, and with every sip, her positive energy resurged. She ate her morning fruit, took a shower, and chose a pink silk suit to wear to church. When she looked in the mirror after getting fully dressed, she felt satisfied. She felt that all was well.

She reached the church parking lot and found a place with ease. She nervously climbed the steps of the church because this was her first time attending, but she had heard positive things about the sermons and choir. She entered and was ushered to a seat. Shortly afterward, the choir softly sang "O Magnify the Lord." Their voices were beautiful, and as she listened to the song, Phoenix felt that things were going to be okay.

Offerings were taken more than once, but Phoenix was thankful that she was able to tip the plate each time it passed. The sermon came from the book of Ecclesiastes and centered on the theme of "casting your bread on the water." The minister was good, and Phoenix took in his every word. After the sermon, he asked those who felt that they needed special prayer to come and kneel before the altar.

As Phoenix rose, someone in the congregation whispered, "Isn't that Phoenix, that girl from the north that works in the library?"

"Chile, I don't know. She looks like her," the other whispered.

"I thought she went to one of them funny churches, new thinking or something?" said the original speaker.

"Yeah, it looks like her," said the other.

"Well, Chile, I don't need prayer, but I'm going to see for myself if that is her up at the altar," said the first speaker.

Phoenix was on her knees asking for forgiveness and direction on her job and in her personal affairs when she felt a huge person push against her and kneel. She readjusted her position at the altar, which took a lot of concentration because she kept picking up negative vibrations. She silently blessed the soul next to her and continued to pray. When the special prayer treatment was over, Phoenix returned to her seat and awaited the service benediction. The choir's last selection was "I've Come Out of the Wilderness."

During the song, tears rolled from the corners of Phoenix's eyes. She felt a release and now knew that she would request an immediate transfer from her place of employment for her own well-being. She left the church knowing that she would go straight home to write a letter to the library administration.

"Chile, there she goes," said the original.

"So it was her," said the other.

"Chile, yeah. I got a good look," said the original.

"Got the nerve to come to our church," said the other.

"I can hardly wait to get home to call my friend, Angel," said the original.

When she reached her apartment, Phoenix sat down on the couch and just reflected for a while. She changed into some comfortable clothes and took a bottle of water from the refrigerator for renewal and started composing a letter in which she gave a few brief descriptions of past incidents. "Professionalism is professionalism," she sighed. She simply wrote the truth. It was Phoenix's only salvation.

She knew that she needed to detach herself from the toxic work environment and the lopsided romantic entanglement. These adverse circumstances had depleted her energy. Something simply had to go so that she could save herself and breathe in new levels of inspiration!

Chapter 8
Trey's Love

Trey reached his car and headed south, straight to the hospital to see Flora. Flora's sister, June, had reached her in time and had updated him on Flora's whereabouts. As he drove, he admitted that he had to be more responsible in choosing women. He had to get beyond the outer beauty and look deeper into the character if he hoped to find a real love match in his life. His thoughts raced and the old song "Bring Me a Higher Love" played on his car radio.

"I take that as a message," he said aloud.

He had never really made a full commitment to anyone because he was unconsciously sending the wrong signals to the universe. He recalled one minister saying that "Your ship hasn't come in because you didn't send one out." And what did he get for a botched request? Flora.

In his college days, he was non-committed and found himself in a situation with the girlfriend that had supported him during the situation with Bill. Her place was his refuge that night, and a few months later, she discovered that she was pregnant. He really adored her, and after she told him what was going on, he started thinking of ways that he could take care of her and a young child.

But before he could share his private plans, she let him know that *she* decided to not keep the child because she did not want to give up her education nor her career plans. He felt cheated and saw that nothing he said would change her mind. The only thing that she wanted from him was for him to drive her to the clinic. She appeared to have everything else under control.

He would never forget the helplessness he felt as he supported her in the ways she requested. He offered financial assistance as well, and she said no. She said that she was prepared to go through with this and shared that she didn't think that he was ready for marriage and fatherhood. This stung!

He was more hurt than he even admitted to himself, but he started choosing to date women who were less headstrong after this experience. He sat there that day in the clinic and fidgeted in his chair, stared at the floor, and studied his hands. He looked at his fingernails and saw things that he'd never noticed before. He counted the squares on the tile on the floor. He squirmed in his seat as he flipped through the women's magazines. He found a half of a stick of gum in his pocket—that was his saving grace. He chewed steadily as he waited for her to emerge from the back. She looked a little weak when she came out, and in the car, she looked straight ahead with a strong resolve with a soft pink scarf tied around her neck. He would not forget how stoic and determined she appeared as he looked over at her from time to time. He did not know what to say to her.

At her place, he sat as she rested. There was minimal conversation, and both knew that this was the end of something. There was a break that could not be mended. He thought they were being careful, but things happen. It had altered his life, and he was facing this turning point in his life for the first time. He then traveled the paths of least resistance when it came to women.

A speeding truck blew his horn, and the noise brought him back to the present moment as he made his way toward Flora. He tightened his seatbelt around his stomach for the courage to face whatever was coming up next. He remembered reading in one of Wayne Dyer's books, *Your Erroneous Zones*, "One was secure whenever they could handle anything that came down the pike." He felt extremely insecure at the thought.

Jeffrey Osborne sang "On the Wings of Love," and Trey briefly imagined being in a relationship with a compatible woman rather than the clingy, insecure woman whom he was going to see.

Lord, he thought, *I know that the excessive pleasure has caused all this pain that we are feeling. I wished that we had taken time to build a better foundation together. Next time, if there is a next time, I will make better choices and, hopefully, attract someone with whom I can at least visualize a future. Maybe she'll calm down if I marry her.*

The more he thought about the idea, the more nauseated he felt. His thoughts continued, *Something just isn't right.* "I need more," he heard himself saying out loud. "I need *more!*" He said with his voice raised as he turned into the hospital parking lot.

Chapter 9

Phoenix's Power

Phoenix was pleased with the letter that she had written, and she rested for a while. The highlights of the sermon had stayed with her awhile, but unfortunately, as night crept in, so did the dark and foreboding thoughts. She was not sure if she could settle with a simple change of jobs.

She had read that when a person outgrows a place or a relationship, nothing seems to cooperate. She continually looked for quick fixes when she realized that perhaps she needed a total change of scenery. The stint in this region had been great, but she also knew that if one overstayed, things would only get worse.

Phoenix felt that something was gnawing at her soul, but she could not put her finger on what was making her feel uncomfortable. She did not feel as though she fit in, and somehow, she could not get to the bottom of things.

There were too many unanswered questions, and there was a shroud of mystery that enveloped the place, which added to her discomfort. She tried to use the affirmation that stated, "None of these things move me," but it only held weight for a season. Her thoughts bombarded her, and she wondered if she would find her comfort zone.

Perhaps she saw through people too well, and it made them uncomfortable. She had seen situations, and people had shared their stories of painful dilemmas, but she was a good steward and did not discuss everything people had shared with her. Immoral relationships and the code of secrecy plagued a number of people who had confided in her. Perhaps the slow pace and the hot weather contributed to the prevalence of these acts. She did not know the answer, but she *did* know that holding it all inside had taken its toll on her.

She reminded herself that God would not give her more than she could handle, so a good outlet for her was often found in creating some prose. She wondered how talk-show hosts and ministers dealt with some of the things that they had to hear. She often wondered how people thought they could actually get away with some of the acts they had committed. Did they not know that the Golden Rule still applied?

She calmed herself and reasserted her power to move forward at the guided and given time. She took solace with her pen and paper and wrote the following verse:

Who's Foolin' Who?

Traveling on the expressway of life,
I had another unexpected blowout.
But in this world of sorrow and strife,
I won't sit around and pout.
People have crises that run deep
'Cause they don't know God at all.
So they try to make others leap
Or keep them blind 'til they fall.
Then they can feel that all is well
And not take responsibility for a solution,
So they try to shut out those who may tell
Of their sadness and sick pollution.
But if eyes are of deep perception
And hearts are of love for God,
Then those with the crises are in deception
'Cause no one can harm a child of God.

Afterward, she ran some bathwater and climbed in for a relaxing soak. She sat in the silence and just listened to guidance and inspiration. She later put on a pair of light-purple pajamas and read the chapter "You are Unburdened" in Mary Kupeferle's *God Will See You Through.* It was just what she needed, and she fell asleep feeling more spiritually empowered.

Chapter 10
Trey's Power

As Trey entered the hospital in an apprehensive state, he stopped at the information desk to find out where Flora was located. He took the elevator, and the ride seemed to last an eternity as he feared what he might see once in her room. When he arrived at the door, he peeked in and saw Flora as she lay there unconscious.

Her mother sat there with her Bible, quietly moving her lips as she obviously read some passage of comfort. She looked like an older version of Flora. Her beauty and smooth skin shone as she sat resolutely. She was a full-figured woman who apparently liked to cook and enjoy good meals.

She looked up at Trey and just nodded, acknowledging his entrance. They had met briefly on two other occasions. She had been at Flora's apartment both times when they were going over new recipes, hanging new draperies, or decorating the apartment.

As he neared the bed, he could see the oxygen machine, which Flora was hooked up to, working diligently. Her sister, June, followed close behind, and there was complete silence and heavy breathing on the part of the spectators. Few words were spoken, but hearts were heavy, and they were all feeling a sense of devastation.

Trey felt light-headed, and after sitting for a period of time, he excused himself. Trey took the elevator downstairs and went to the lobby shop to purchase cigarettes. The brands were limited, so he had to settle for a very strong brand, and he paid dearly for them.

He went to the exit and stood outside with the other wretched visitors who had a need to light up. He puffed a bit and felt even dizzier and more unsteady. He snuffed it out and floated back inside. He sat in the lobby and just stared with a vacant look. He looked around and noted that most of the other people sitting around looked as if they were in a zone as they stared into space.

He returned to the room and walked over and kissed Flora lightly on the forehead. He took a seat, and after a long silence, Flora's mother started talking. "When she was a little girl, Flora always seemed to grasp too tightly to things. She had a problem with letting people go and often read too much into situations. Don't feel *too* badly, son. This is not the first time this has happened. She has done it before in the name of *love*." Her mother breathed deeply.

Trey raised his head and looked at Flora's mother with a sidelong glance. "How come I did not know this?" he whispered hoarsely.

"Well, Trey, no one goes around sharing all of their or their family's past history. I think that Flora was under the impression that you would be her future husband, and because she's in her midthirties, I feel she had begun to feel desperate," her mother added.

"Is she going to make it?"

"The doctors say that they believe she will pull through, provided that she has a lot coaxing, love, and understanding," her sister responded.

"I feel so guilty," offered Trey. "I simply missed calling her from the conference on time. I did not realize that the situation was *this* sensitive. No one ever told me of any past suicide attempts. I am baffled, and I am confused.

"Oh Lord! Well, I can make it up to her if she will just get well. When she regains consciousness, I'll ask her to be my wife," he heard this strange voice say. He couldn't believe that these words had come from his own lips. Trey asked to be excused.

June assured him that she wouldn't be coming around for another twenty-four hours due to heavy sedatives. He walked over and kissed the lukewarm Flora again on the forehead then dizzily floated from the hospital room. As he descended on the elevator, everything was a blur to him. Everybody's voice seemed muffled. He couldn't make sense of anything at that point. He walked briskly out into the cool breeze and headed toward his car.

The Exit sign was one of the best things that he had seen that day. When he reached his apartment, he opened the door feeling a sense of power as he let out a sigh. "Thank God."

He dropped his luggage and undressed and wrapped his purple robe around him. He went and looked in the refrigerator and was glad to see that there was a bottle of wine. He poured a glass and sat in his favorite chair, and after his second glass of wine, he heard himself saying out loud, "Did I really promise Flora's folks I'd marry her? Oh my god! What is going to become of me?"

The more he thought of Flora, he knew something was not right. "It's like I can't feel her depth. I don't know how far she will take things. I cannot read her, and the more I think about it, I feel unsteady when I am with her. I can't feel her soul, so it makes me feel as though I am wavering and off base." He knew that he had made his bed, so he had to lie in it until the tides changed. Until then, he knew that he had to master himself first and appeal to the higher angels to guide him as he continued to listen for divine instruction.

Chapter 11

Phoenix's Imagination

Phoenix took the letter to the library administration office and sent a copy through Express Mail from the downtown post office. She had Monday off, and on Tuesday, she started to get ready to return to her job, which she now equated to a war zone. She silently hoped that the library administrators had heard her desperate plea for a transfer for either Angel or for herself. She wanted to finish what she had started in helping the neighborhood children see themselves in a more positive light by exposing them to books with characters that looked like them. There was so much she wanted to share, but she knew that the outcome was uncertain.

After her morning meditation along with her coffee, Phoenix felt that she could and would handle whatever came and hoped to remain calm in the process. She arrived at work on time—and on the day there was to be a series of workshops. Several of her former coworkers from a local college were coming to speak to the parents about early reading intervention.

Phoenix wanted to make a good impression and certainly did not want her guests to see what was really going on at the library. She boldly went into the library, and when she spoke, the two sitting at the desk said nothing. "Okay," she said inaudibly. This along with the fact that Angel was in her parking spot let her know the tone of the day.

Phoenix went to her desk. She opened the book she had recently purchased called *The Snow White Syndrome* by Betsy Cohen. She stopped to read the following passage:

Envy is hostility, the withholding of friendship, hate stares, snubs, ridicule, cattiness, whispering, troublemaking, calumny, sulking, silence, acting injured, as if someone actually did something to hurt you. Its uncalled-for temper tantrums, like slamming things down, walking very fast with heels banging on the floor (very common, like the woman who huffs and puffs . . .

It was so perfect for what she was experiencing, so she wrote it down verbatim and taped it to the leaflet on her desk. It seemed to be the right thing to do to express what she lived through on a daily basis. She also felt that it might help future staff cope.

The library opened, and several of her favorite patrons came in to chat briefly. It was as if they could feel that something was happening. But then, she knew they knew. The community always knows. Shortly after those chats, a chief library administrator from the central office walked in, asked to speak with Phoenix, and informed her that she was being transferred immediately to another branch. He said that she would be on a new six-month probationary period and told her where she would be reporting. It all happened so fast that Phoenix informed the head librarian that she wanted to take a walk around the community.

She left the library and started walking through the impoverished yet sainted neighborhood. She cried as she looked at the community children outside playing, who so sorely needed love and guidance. She walked on as the tears flowed, and instinctively, she ended up at one of the local elementary schools. She headed toward the school library and the school librarian in the hallway. They had worked together in the past. She took one look at Phoenix and knew that a disaster had taken place.

The school librarian took Phoenix aside and kept reminding her that it was for the best. After Phoenix calmed down, she could hear the children singing from the music room. They were singing "You'll Never Walk Alone." It gave her the strength to leave the school and return to the library.

After having been gone for about an hour, Phoenix walked back slowly to what she equated with the temple of doom. She returned to the library through the back door. She basically kept to herself, and everyone could see that it was the best thing to do. They could see the mixture of daggers and pain in her eyes. Only a complete fool would rush in now.

Finally, the speakers showed up for the workshops that were being given for the neighborhood parents. The events were well attended, and Phoenix was able to maintain her poise and composure through it all. After the last guest speaker finished packing up her presentation items, Phoenix told her she would walk her to her car and help her with her presentation items.

They stood there and chatted for a few moments, and after the woman drove off, Phoenix attempted to reenter the library. The door was locked. She tried the front, but the gate was down. She knocked for a while, and eventually, Angel finally let her in.

Phoenix quietly went over to her desk with an empty box, cleaned out her files, and put her plant on top. The other staff members stood quietly as though they had tears in their eyes, as if to say, "We didn't want you to leave. We just enjoy taunting you. We don't read, and we like the drama. All we have to do is agitate and view."

Phoenix put the box in her car, turned the ignition, put the car in reverse, and never looked back. She drove and pressed on toward home and confirmed, "This is the day for ending things. I've got one more situation to handle to close out this phase of my life." As she cruised home, she knew she had to verify the mysteries of her love life as well. She was ready to "take out *all* the garbage."

She drove in silence, and the farther she got away from the scene, the lighter she felt. As the street widened in the more prosperous area of the street, her visions and hope expanded as well. She reached the university area, and by that time, she started singing a spiritual she had written many years ago, "That's the Lord working in you favor, so just cool out and thank the Lord."

She didn't bother to bring her box of files up. She just put them in the trunk for the next assignment. She only brought up her plant to water it and give it light. She straightened up some and listened to some smooth jazz in an effort to relax. She popped open a can of beer and mumbled, "Still got some more unfinished business."

As she finished the beer, she decided to check out the inevitable. Was her best friend really sleeping with her guy? She simply had to know! It was now dark, and these dark thoughts loomed. She knew that she should not be investigating, but all reasoning could not stop her. She headed to her car and drove to his house, and it was almost as if the car was being driven by an invisible force.

She'd made that journey so many times before, and her car, Tawny, seemed to know the way on its own. When she got there, having just turned the bend, there sat Lila's new Jaguar in the driveway. She paused. She didn't know what to do. She sat there for a while with the old car idling a little loudly. Then she pulled into the driveway behind Lila's car. Her thoughts raced. *Should I ring the bell and turn this place out or should I just let it go?*

She sat there for a while. She did not see any lights on inside and figured they did not even know she was out there. She sat and cried and wondered if she should ring the bell. But in a mess of tears, Phoenix decided to back out instead, and in a nervous zigzag, she ended up taking a part of his sidewalk mailbox with her. He then ran out the house still buckling the belt on his pants, shouting, "I'll call the police!"

She just sped off confused, moving in a fog. She forgot about where she was headed and just drove and drove. She wasn't ready to go home yet and stew. But the more she drove, the more unfamiliar her surroundings became.

She thought that she knew the city quite well, but now she knew that she was *really* lost. She knew she was in trouble when she ended up on a dark two-lane highway that was heading into the state of Mississippi. When she saw two big white corner posts on both sides of the highway and a plantation-looking house to the right, she realized that she was truly headed for trouble. It was like a surreal picture of an entry into the pearly gates.

Phoenix quickly did a three-point turn and drove in the opposite direction until she saw lights and civilization. When she saw houses and residential districts again, her bladder began to scream for alleviation. She pulled over to the side of a street and, hoping that no one was looking, took a long, long leak.

Luckily, she was not stopped. She returned to the steering wheel and saw a Pizza Hut in a strip mall. The lights were still on. She staggered to the door. It was locked, but a young teenager came to the door and said that they were closed. She asked for directions back to the city, and the young woman pointed her in the proper direction. She was her angel for that night, which was filled with pain, fear, and terror.

As Phoenix put the car in reverse, her hand accidentally hit the volume controls on the radio, and the song "Faith that Conquers Anything" was playing. She had forgotten that the radio was still on and turned down low. She knew then that there were truly angels watching over her, and the Holy Spirit was guiding her to safety.

She found her bearings and reached her place. She trudged up the stairs to her apartment, and her neighbor downstairs opened her door and said, "Are you okay?"

Phoenix thanked Cathy, responding, "Not really, but thanks. Thanks for looking out, Cathy," she said in a low voice.

She turned the key to her apartment, entered, and quietly sat down on the couch and realized how close she had come to real danger. She stretched out and threw her light-blue throw over herself and dozed off. She imagined that she was in the arms of someone who truly cared and could bring a level of comfort. She recalled how this guy never wanted to hear some of the things that plagued her; he only reminded her of what he did not like about her, including her drinking.

She remembered saying to him, "Then let me tell you about some of the things that are bothering me." He responded, "I can't deal with your emotions." So Phoenix now understood that someone who not only could but wanted to know what was going on with her would appear. As Septima used to say to her, "Error coming to the surface to be removed." She gained a sense of peace as she felt that she was being raised for a higher-leveled union with someone of like mind.

Chapter 12

Trey's Imagination

Trey woke up in his bed but didn't remember getting into bed. He thanked his higher power for taking over. He rubbed his eyes and sat up, and the first thing he saw was the blinking light on his phone. He hesitated before retrieving the message. He first went and washed his face, brushed his teeth, and put on some coffee. He pushed play and heard the sharp voice of his department chairman telling him to report at 8:00 a.m. sharp on Monday to explain why he had quit the annual literary conference. He felt sickened all over again and realized that his troubles were far from over. He had about three days before he had to face the lion's roar.

He lazily sat around and sipped on his coffee. He read through a few inspirational books to try and get centered before going back through the hospital ordeal. The thought of marrying Flora made him feel uneasy, but what could he say. His world, his mess.

He put on comfortable clothes after showering and headed for the hospital. He had taken two aspirins to counteract the prior day's craziness. Trey arrived at the hospital fully expecting to see a repeat scene of the day before, but to his surprise, Flora was sitting up in bed. He stood there in shock, remembering to close his mouth. He closed it and sat down. Her mother, seated to the right of the bed, said, "The doctors say it's a miracle."

"Yes, it is," said Trey.

"Hi, Trey, darling. Mother told me that you proposed to me while I was sleeping." Flora smiled. "I feel like sleeping beauty."

"Well, I, I—" he stammered.

"That makes me feel so much *more* secure knowing that I'll have you to take care of me. Then we can make sure that I don't get that uptight about living again," she cooed.

Trey thought he would end up in the empty bed next to Flora when he began to feel faint. Instead, he just sat down in the empty chair feeling depleted.

"The doctors said that I can go home tomorrow if I agree to counseling. I agreed," she added.

Her mother rose and said, "Flora, I will be at home. I need some rest, dear." She left after kissing her on the forehead and merely patting Trey on the back as she left the room.

Trey sat a while and said very little. He was glad that she had on the television so he could escape by looking at the news shows and not at her.

"Okay," said Trey after a couple of hours. "I'll be here to pick you up in the morning."

"Oh," she said, holding up a pen and pad. "I'm already getting our wedding plans together. I want June to be the maid of honor and—"

"Flora," Trey interrupted, "let us discuss this when you are back home and feeling better."

"Well, okay." Her voice shifted like a rejected child. "If you say so . . ." She trailed off.

When the nurse came in to change her linen, he stepped out. He went down to smoke some of the strong cigarettes he had bought the day before. He leaned against the wall outside, drew in, and blew out. Again, after feeling his head spin, he floated back inside to return to Flora's room.

Upon returning, he eased in. "I will be here in the morning to pick you up. I have a lot to do today," said Trey.

"Like what?" her voice hardened.

"Like try to figure out what the hell is going on in my life!" his voice strengthened.

"Trey, why are you talking to me like this?" she whined. "You know that I'm sick and don't feel like an argument."

"Flora, my damn job is on the line because you pulled a crazy-assed stunt like *this*, and you're just going to act like you came down with a mere headache or cold?" he spoke through his teeth.

"Nurse! Nurse!" she screamed and began to push the nurse station button.

"Okay, okay, okay. Calm down. Calm down." He softened.

The nurse came in and said that they would have to ask him to leave because he was upsetting the patient. He stormed out talking to himself, saying "Upsetting the patient, upsetting the patient" repeatedly. He walked to his car talking to himself.

One approaching couple just moved over and gave each other a look as if to say "there goes a madman." He found his car, turned the ignition, and just sat there for what seemed like hours. He regained his sense of equilibrium and chose to go to the lakefront to soothe his thoughts.

Once there, he pulled up at the beach where he saw children playing and was reminded of how safe and simple life was back then. "We take so much for granted. We never realize what our parents go through simply to keep a family together. Whew!"

He sat in the car awhile and watched the birds flying freely and admired the beauty of the blue Lake Michigan. It was a dry and sunny day, and he just sat and sat and peered out over the horizon.

The next day, Trey picked up Flora, who looked as though nothing had happened at all. All he could see were her sculptured nails, and it dawned on him just how little substance this woman actually had. He couldn't forget how frightening this had been and now wondered what she was truly capable of doing. *How far would she go?*

However, he had promised himself that he would be patient, kind, and loving—and all the things his mother had taught him to be when dealing with womanhood. He had to take responsibility for the part that he had played in this whole ordeal.

They reached her apartment where the incident had taken place, and he noted that things were in disarray, which signified her confused state. He pampered her and put clean sheets on the bed. He ran a tub of water and gently helped her to bed.

Afterward, he rolled up his sleeves and started to straighten up the place, and as he did so, he started to see Flora in a whole different light. He again noticed that there were no books except for a few magazines on fashion, beauty, skin care, and weddings. Most of her music choices were sad love songs, which contributed to her state of mind.

He recalled that whenever he came here, Flora always had a spread that looked like something out of a cooking class, and she had a lot of cookbooks. Falling into her net had been fairly easy because of the spicy smells, good foods, and the way she appeared to always be in agreement with whatever he wanted to do.

The more he thought about it, she had done most of the calling—and most of the giving. The ever-ready food and sexy lingerie helped bait him. She came along at a time when he thought that this was what he really wanted. She was far from his college girlfriend who challenged him on many levels—she let it be known that she was neither his servant nor cook, and they usually ate out, played chess or Scrabble, and there was a lot of mental sparing.

"Again, taking folks for granted," he heard himself say. Now he really missed her.

"Trey," he heard the voice from the other room, "are you on the phone?"

"No, Flora," he said flatly.

"But I heard you say something," she continued.

"Just rest, dear." He tried to soften. *Maybe,* he thought, careful not to speak out loud, *I can interest her in some of the activities I used to enjoy.* He tried to convince himself. *Maybe it'll work out.*

That night, Trey spent the night at Flora's. He held her all night to relax her and assure her things would be all right, even though he didn't know if he would be all right. He had even gone to his apartment and fixed up a big packet of activities for them. They all turned her off, and she said that she just wanted him to hold her and make love to her. Days passed. Little changed.

Trey began to feel more helpless, caught, and betrayed by life. He was glad when Sunday morning came because he knew that he was going to attend church and hear a sermon. At this point, any words of encouragement would be welcome words. He invited her, and as expected, she said no. She was not interested because she didn't want the people staring at her.

"But, Flora, they do not even know you," he had said.

Then she said that she did not like that church. He asked her if she had ever been there, and she said no, but that a friend of hers did not like it. He winced.

Relieved to be leaving her apartment but sickened about his predicament, he hurried home and got ready for church. Just when he felt he was ready to leave, he started to feel heavyhearted, and he sat down. Before he even realized it, he started to cry. He hadn't done this since his mother had passed. But once he started, he couldn't stop, and finally, he pulled himself together and told himself that perhaps he needed to release it all. He decided not to be defeated, and he made himself go on to the church.

The sermon was dynamic! He thought about one line from the sermon which was on love. The minister had asked, "Would you want to marry you?" He also spoke of the biblical passage, which spoke of "couples being equally yoked." Both gave him a lot to ponder.

Once home again, he relaxed and curled up with one of Dickens's novels, *The Pickwick Papers*. He had just gotten to the part about the club keeping bad company when the phone rang.

"Trey, how was church?" Flora cooed.

"Great," responded Trey.

"I feel much better, and I cooked some chicken Parmesan and—"

"Flora," he interrupted, "I'm going to eat here today."

"Aw, so you're expecting someone, huh?" she retorted.

"No, Flora. If you'd like to come over for an inspection, you're more than welcome, but I'm not leaving the apartment again today," he added.

She altered and said, "That's okay, Trey. I am sorry if I sounded like I was accusing you. I guess I'm just not feeling as well as I should. I'll talk to you later, okay?"

"Okay," he responded. He thought to himself, *Sounds like you feel like your old self again.* After that, he cut off the ringer and put on the answering machine to screen his calls. He retired early after rehearsing his notes on what he would say to his supervisor about quitting the conference.

That Monday morning, his supervisor spoke of how he had let the panel and the whole department down. He could not understand what would incline Trey to make such an irresponsible move. For job purposes and excusal for such behavior, he had to admit that his girlfriend had attempted suicide. He felt like dying in front of this man, but he knew that it could be investigated, so he told the truth.

He was dismissed from a book committee that he had waited to be a part of, and he bravely faced the consequences of his actions. He left the English department; it seemed that the office staff studied him for a visible reaction. Luckily, a good friend and coworker caught him by the arm and said, "Hey, Trey. Let's do lunch." She could see that he needed a friend.

He agreed and told her that the treat was on him. They said they'd meet in the faculty parking lot at high noon. At the prescribed time, each drove and met at a nearby restaurant where a lot of the university employees hung out and talked shop. Sandy, his coworker, had a knack for picking up on other people's pain and always seemed to be in the right place at the right time to come to the rescue.

She was married and was just a good person to know and could make others laugh when the job became too much. After gorging down Reuben sandwiches and laughing at job stuff, they noted the time and knew that it was time to return to work.

As Sandy was about to enter the driver's side of her car, a person lunged from behind another car and began to verbally attack Sandy. Trey rushed around to the other side of the car, but he was too slow because, by then, Sandy was leaning against the car gasping for air.

"Bitch, stay away from my fiancé! You were the reason he wouldn't answer the phone last night."

After Trey pulled Flora away from Sandy, who was an asthmatic, Sandy searched nervously in her purse for her inhaler and car keys. She was shaking as she got inside her car, inhaled from her pipe, and finally talked herself through starting the car and putting it in reverse to escape the madness of the moment. Trey waved for her to drive on, and she sped off.

He dragged Flora with a bear grip by her shoulders to his own car, and once he had gotten her inside, he went and got in the driver's seat. They both sat there breathing like wild animals, trying to catch their breaths. Trey sat there and tried to imagine being in a relationship with a sane person.

Then, as his breathing slowed, he silently asked God to guide him and help him to redeem and purify himself. He could see that these were the consequences of his getting his appetites satisfied in this relationship. He now knew that it was *not* enough and even dangerous. He needed a higher and more spiritual union with someone but did not see how that could happen at this juncture. All he *could* see was Flora's head leaning back on the light-blue headrest as she whimpered like a disobedient child who had been caught in the wrong.

Chapter 13
Phoenix's Understanding

Anxious thoughts filled Phoenix's mind when she awakened and realized that she no longer worked at that library. Thank goodness she had three days before the new assignment started, so she had time to adjust her thinking. At this point, she was not feeling that optimistic because she was not sure that her system-wide contributions had been noticed. Angel had not been questioned for her antics and was allowed to stay at her location due to seniority. "That's the way of the world," she breathed out.

She started her day with her normal rituals of having coffee, journaling, and reading some spiritual literature to fortify herself for the day. She felt that things were coming along as they should, and she started to feel more tranquil. One line from Mary Baker Eddy's writings said, "Never breathe an immoral atmosphere unless in an attempt to purify it." With that thought, she relaxed and realized that she could not purify that situation and was glad that she had been graciously removed.

She decided to go down to the river. Looking at the water helped her relax. But first, she called her boyfriend and asked him if he was seeing Lila. He said he did not know what she was talking about and asked if she had been drinking. She ended the conversation with this line: "Every time you touch someone else, you lose a degree of me. One day you will understand." Then she hung up. She saw just how shallow he was!

At the river, she remained in her car and listened to some smooth jazz and love songs, and she sat and watched the sun shine from the pier. She envisioned herself making the journey across the bridge and heading home. "This situation is breaking my spirit. There are just too many negative forces coming from too many directions," she mumbled. She left the river with a clearer resolve of what she had to do. She had to go.

She returned home and cleaned her apartment and organized papers in an attempt to get ready for her new assignment. The day passed, but as night fell, feelings of insecurity and fear crept in. She had hung with her longtime friend, Joel Goldsmith's *The Art of Meditation*, for portions of the evening. Usually, one or two lines from the chapter "Fear Not" helped her relax and trust the process.

The more she thought about it, she knew that did not have the energy to meet a whole new staff nor start building new trenches. She did not think that she could muster the strength to continue to build on quicksand. She called her minister, and they talked. Phoenix poured out her heart, and afterward, she felt hopeful. She could see glimmers of hope.

Her minister said, "Perhaps you should try to leave this place, Phoenix. It's like an old pair of shoes that have worn out their usefulness. Let it go. Ask for guidance. Stop clutching and groping. Loose it, and let it go."

With these thoughts in mind, Phoenix said, "Out of ashes, peace will rise," which exemplified the meaning of the Indian belief of the phoenix. Her mother had named her after the phoenix, a bird that was known to represent the sun and to renew itself daily. She felt it was time to live up to the name and be wise enough to follow the best path for her life.

Her ideas raced. *Where will I get the money to leave?* she wondered. *What will I do with my furniture?* As the doubts bombarded her, she was determined to find a way and to get out. Walls were closing in on her, but she knew herself well enough to know that she had to chart her own destiny.

"Forget everything and everybody," she said. "It's about me this time. I am independent of what others think. That is the only way I will get to the other side—alive!" she vowed.

Phoenix understood that it was truly time to let go. She released all concerns, removed her gold earrings, and she lay down on the couch. "Gotta go! Nothing else matters! Then I can turn over several new leaves," she affirmed gently.

Chapter 14
Trey's Understanding

Trey was upset about his circumstances with his job on the line. It was his livelihood, and he not only needed to support himself, but now it looked as though he would be caring for Flora as well. He also hoped that Sandy would not press charges against Flora after the verbal lashing that had sent her into an asthmatic attack.

He now knew that he was paying dues for his poor choices. As the old song went, "Nothing from nothing leaves nothing." He was reaping a sparse crop from his selfish and limited sowing in this relationship.

He couldn't keep telling the office that he had personal problems. They only cared up to an extent, and then he needed to get help or move on. That's the way of the world. Compassion only goes so far, but when it started cutting into business, then it became a hardship to all concerned.

How could he get it across to Flora that she could not continue to call him at work at every whim? Nor could she go on attacking his professional colleagues who shared no romantic interests in him. Did she get it? Did not she understand that if there is no income, there is little room for their happiness? Was she thinking beyond her own insecure moment?

And how could he face Sandy at work? What should he do? Should he wear a sign saying, "Excuse me. I slept with a madwoman! Watch your back because you might get attacked!" Trey sat on the side of his bed with his head in both hands. He was filled with fear and despair as he thought about the upcoming meeting at work. He snapped out of his dark thoughts when the phone started ringing. He hesitated before reaching for it to steel his nerves. He picked it up and cautiously said, "Hello?"

"Hi, Trey," Flora said.

"Yes," he answered.

"I've got some news for you," Flora cooed sweetly.

"Yes, Flora," he answered in a mechanical way.

"I hope that you are sitting down," she said, grinning.

"I am, Flora," he said.

"I just found out . . ." Her voice seemed to become fainter.

"What, Flora?" he asked, his voice raised.

"You don't have to scream, Trey. I just wanted to tell you that we're having a *baby*," she said emphatically.

"We're having a what?" his voice grew louder. "*A baby?*"

"Trey, I just found out that I'm pregnant, and it's good that the accident did not harm the baby!" she exclaimed.

Trey just held the phone. *The accident,* he thought. "Flora," he heard himself say, "can I call you back? I was in the middle of something."

"*What?*" she snapped. "In the middle of what?"

"Flora," he raised his voice with authority, "I said that I'll call you back!" he screamed.

Floored again by Flora, Trey put the phone on the hook. His hands were trembling, his back was hurting down the center, and he felt his left eye twitching at regular intervals. Here he had a stack of seventy-five compositions to grade, and now this.

Pregnant! His mind started racing. *She said she was on the pill. She said she had used the diaphragm.* "Oh hell," he said out loud. "She said. She said! Stupid me."

Trey stood looking out of his high-rise apartment in total disbelief. He peered out over the calm lake and felt like he needed to run and maybe even see if a plunge would help clear his head. The weather would not permit the latter, but he did need to soothe his inner turbulence.

He threw on his jogging suit and running shoes and took an extra jacket. Though the weather was brisk, he took the elevator down, walked over to the lakefront, and broke into a breakneck speed as though something or someone was chasing him. He ran and ran until other more regular-paced joggers looked at him as he passed. They could detect that he had the momentum of a person with a problem. He did indeed!

As he ran, he thought of all his past dealings with women. He took a look inside his own mind and came face-to-face with some hard truths. None of his relationships had ever seemed to turn out right. He had to admit that he had not given himself fully since the college sweetheart and only had himself to blame for some of the outcomes. "Next time, if there is a next time, I need a woman who prays. I know that people develop spiritually at different paces, but she must first get on the path. I am on the path to higher understanding, and if I survive this, I will either try to enlighten Flora or pray for someone who can relate to where I am and where I want to go with my life."

He remembered the college sweetheart who chose to terminate rather than feel like she was stagnating. He never fully admitted even to how powerless he felt or how helpless to offer her a better set of circumstances at that phase in their lives. But now he had to face the fact that he felt crushed and privately locked off a part of his heart. She thought that he was somewhat aloof and cool and had no idea how much he ached inside.

After that, he had basically dealt with women with little substance yet good looks; he felt that he'd have a greater chance for having the upper hand in the relationship, and he could give of himself only marginally.

But now—Flora. *Beautiful but limited. And lately, the beauty had begun to fade,* he thought. His pace slowed, and he eventually came to a stop. He looked back and could not believe how far he had run.

"Payback is a dog," he sighed. "Lord," he said as he looked up into the dismal gray, sunless sky. "Lord, I need your help," he pleaded.

He found a patch of grass and sat down as he panted. Tears rolled down, and they seemed endless. They would not stop. He had his back to the streets because he did not want anyone to witness a grown man in crying mode. He was glad that he had a neck towel around his neck, which also served as a handkerchief. He let it all hang out and threw in all reasons for crying, such as missing his mother, having to marry Flora, and the possibility of losing his job. He waited for the pain to subside, and when he felt stronger, he walked over to a rock. He sat and looked out over the horizon feeling shipwrecked.

He slowly came around. He hoped that no one had seen this breakdown, and he got up and walked toward the apartment at a slow pace. He carefully placed one foot in front of the other as he had learned as a child. He had one revelation that gave him hope.

"I'm going to call my father," he audibly proclaimed. "I know what he's going to say, but I need him. I'm already prepared for the 'I told you, son. Don't sleep with a woman you wouldn't want to marry.'"

But still, he'll understand. He was a young man once, and surely, he had to acquire that wisdom from his own mistakes. He understood that becoming a husband and a father were inevitable, much to his dismay. He walked toward his place and wiped his face with the gold towel to clear his view of what lay ahead.

Chapter 15

Phoenix's Will

Phoenix could see that her future ahead would brighten only if she took action. This had been a great place to slow down and heal after losing her father, but it was clear that it was time to move on. A cycle had ended, and only she was responsible for reading her own intuitive messages. Listening to others could only derail her life.

The silent forces were pulling her northward, and she was taking notice of what she was hearing. She had grown and prospered here as well as matured immensely. Even she could see that. She had a new degree and professional experience to add to her resume. She knew she'd better leave while the gains were intact and marketable.

Ready to move forward, Phoenix took action and got on the phone to check moving, storage, and traveling costs. She envisioned herself driving across the mighty Mississippi and heading home to Chicago. The Hindus found rivers to be sacred, and the river had sustained her on many occasions, but she was ready to be around the blue lake at this juncture. She was ready for a cool change. "Whew!" she blew out. "I need to breathe," she stated emphatically.

Phoenix called her mother, Septima. She cried about her situation, and her mother listened patiently. She advised her to read the Psalm 91 until she felt protected and guided. After the phone conversation ended, she went and got her Bible and read Psalm 91 three times. The words soaked in, and Phoenix gradually rose from the couch and retrieved an empty box that she had been saving.

She placed a few books in it and knew that this was just the beginning of turning her vision into reality. She worked for a while until the ringing of the phone stopped her.

She rose to answer it and heard "Aunt Phoenix?"—as her aunt affectionately called her. "Your mother said you needed money to get out of there. How much do you need?"

"Aunt Louise?" Phoenix's voice quaked. "I need $500." She trembled. This was her father's only sister who was also known as the stingy one. She couldn't believe her ears.

"Okay! I'm having someone give it to the postman. I pray it will reach you by Monday so you can get the hell out of there. I heard that they treat you bad if you're a Yankee down there. Your father never wanted you to go in the first place. He worried a lot about you being down there. I'm getting old, and I need you to help me up here. Bye, and I love you," her aunt closed.

Phoenix sat in the middle of the floor and cried tears of joy. First, there was disbelief, but that changed to belief. "Answered prayer!" she exclaimed. She phoned her older sister on the West Coast and told her what had happened.

"You mean that witch came through! Call me when it gets there!" her sister said as she laughed.

That Saturday, Phoenix sang as she packed. She talked to as few people as possible about her decisions because she knew that they would try to change her mind. Her mind was made up, and no old forces or old lovers were going to convince her otherwise.

She knew that she'd have to leave her furniture in storage—as the saying goes, "If you want to travel far, you have to travel light." The main thing was to get herself out. Material things could be replaced, but her soul could not!

She would just take enough temporary items for survival such as her clothes, spiritual books and books for work, her degree, and mainly her mind, body, and soul to higher ground.

Phoenix went to buy more boxes, and as she drove, she listened to music other than spirituals, which was a sign of her relaxing. She heard a few love songs and faintly thought of trying love again, but that had to wait.

She stopped by her aunt and uncle's house, and her uncle checked out her car. It was old, and she had bought it before coming there. If cars could talk, Tawny—that was her car's name—would have interesting tales to tell. Her uncle ended their conversation by saying that she could make it on a "wing and a prayer."

Movers put her items in a storage bin for safekeeping, and Phoenix chose to spend her last Sunday by going to see her minister and spending time with her. They talked and she said her good-byes, and well wishes came from others in the congregation. Everything seemed to be falling into place, and now she only had to wait for the check from her aunt.

As she awakened to the warmth of the Southern heat and the chirping of the birds, Phoenix realized it was Monday. After drinking her coffee, she slowly went to the mailbox, and there was this barely legible letter addressed to her. It was from her eighty-year-old aunt who always put Scotch tape across the written lines, she guessed for safeguarding.

When she opened the envelope, there was a check. It was written upside down, so to speak. Where it had "pay to the order," her Aunt Louise had written "$500"; and on the line where the dollar amount was supposed to go, there was Phoenix's name.

"Oh, hell!" Phoenix quibbled out loud. "I wonder if the bank will cash it. Will they pull that ten-day waiting period for out-of-state checks? Will they make her re-issue it?"

But due to glorious miracles, the young teller found it rather amusing and put it through with no problem. Phoenix took care of all outstanding business and decided to spend her last night with her aunt and uncle. They totally welcomed the idea.

She dropped off her letter of resignation at the library headquarters. She found this to be one of the easiest things on her *to do* list. She smiled all the way back to her car. Things were working like clockwork. She knew that when it was time to go, it was time to go.

She enjoyed her aunt and uncle and left their home about 5:00 a.m. with her aunt and uncle's blessings. She finally drove across the bridge that she had watched so many days while watching the setting sun by the riverside. She followed that Northern Star. Though it was not visible to the eye, it was truly visible to her heart. She drove north on what southerners called the double-nickel, meaning I-55. She drove, and all seemed well. She stopped at the halfway point, the family stop-off, which is Mt. Vernon, Illinois. There, her car started steaming when she stopped to gas up. A couple of mechanics were available.

One said, "Miss, how far are you going?"

"To Chicago," she answered.

He looked in the direction of Chicago and looked really worried. Then the two mechanics just looked at each other. They did the best they could to repair the busted hose, and both probably whispered a prayer. But as her uncle had vowed, she would make it on a wing and a prayer. She continued her journey.

When she approached the bridge that crosses over into Illinois, she took a deep breath. She drove up the incline, which seemed unusually high to her on that day. She felt fearful because it seemed so steep. Her cousins had made a CD, and the music on it gave her the confidence to complete the journey. Her cousin Nita sang "Sparc Me, One Moment of the Day," while her brother Chris backed her up on an electric guitar. Listening to them gave her the grit she needed.

Halfway across the bridge, Phoenix saw the sign that read "Illinois State Line." She said loudly, "Thank you, God! Thank you, God! *Thank you*, God!" She held up her diploma in her free right hand and shouted, Yes! The next sign said, "The People of Illinois Welcome You." She smiled and felt the sign was truly sincere. She forged ahead, thankful that the trials had not consumed her and knowing that her prayers, patience, and persistence had truly paid off.

Chapter 16
Trey's Will

Trey headed toward his father's house, and once he entered onto the expressway heading south, he began to breathe more freely. He exhaled some of the stifling thoughts and inhaled more positive ones. It was a Sunday afternoon, and he knew his father, Elisha, would be home from church by the time he traveled from the far north side to his home in the southern suburbs. He was glad that his father had adapted to a more relaxed lifestyle, and it suited him well.

He started to turn on the radio but decided to relish the silence as he concentrated on the upcoming conversation. He would just state the facts and tell what happened and let the chips fall where they may fall.

Elisha was a widower and retired from the post office. He always reminded Trey that he was expected to go further and do better. Trey knew that his parents had sacrificed greatly for his education. And they had sacrificed the ultimate-personal happiness—to make sure Trey had a stable home environment.

He had learned after his mother's death that there was a private lifetime battle going on between his parents. Elisha had had a brief affair with a teacher, and his mother would not let him live it down. She brought it up over the years as the quencher when the battles were deeply engrossed. It always guaranteed her victory as far as having the last word.

Trey didn't know the details, but he knew that there was a deep rift in the marriage. Elisha truly loved this woman, and they had a lot in common, including the love of books and knowledge. This had intimidated his mother, Rose, who was never into books. She was a great homemaker as far as cooking and cleaning, and she did eventually get a job to help with the bills. But she never had a love or acquired a love for the printed word.

But they had lived through it; yet he sometimes wondered if his mother's inability to forgive contributed to her illness. They had so many years together after the affair, and the cheating happened very early in the marriage. He wished that his mother could have moved on in her own heart, and maybe she would still be alive.

A huge tractor trailer blew at him, and he swerved back into his lane, realizing that he needed to focus on driving and on his own grim situation with Flora. But the present seemed too difficult to face, so he reflected on the days with his former girlfriend for a while. He had let her slip away and had heard that she had married well to a stand-up guy. She had called him before her wedding and expressed her condolences in regard to his mother.

She also told him that she'd always have a special place in her heart for him. She said that she realized that their lives had to take different paths and that she asked for his blessings for her upcoming marriage. During the conversation, he basically listened and said little. Afterward, he went to what was then a local pub and drank too much. He later heard through the grapevine that she was doing fine and had given birth to a beautiful little girl.

Shortly afterward, Trey went to a new Ethiopian restaurant for lunch on the north side to ease his thoughts. There were not many people inside the restaurant. He noticed an extremely attractive woman dining alone. She smiled at him, and he returned the smile and went on to his table.

As he began to roll his vegetables into the specially made bread, he looked up when he heard a soft voice ask, "Are you alone?"

"Yes." He swallowed.

"Expecting anyone?" she cooed.

"No." He gulped.

"Mind if I join you?" Flora asked.

"No," he said hesitantly.

"I just didn't want to get depressed as I ate alone," she volunteered.

That was how he met Flora, who continued to be very forward, often unhappy. "I should have known to run then," Trey said under his breath.

He exited the expressway and entered the town of Matteson. Trey slowed down, and when he reached his father's home, he pulled into the driveway. He turned off the ignition and just sat for a while. He hoped that he could bide his time before entering and be given the power to say the right thing.

Elisha sat by the window in his recliner. He looked out and silently opened his Bible to Psalm 27. He sighed. *My boy is in serious trouble*, he thought, and he slowly read as he waited for Trey to enter. They both needed a moment to allow themselves to prepare for what was to come.

Trey's father usually exuded calmness just as the biblical prophet after whom he was named. His father was also diplomatic, and it took a lot to make him really angry. However, when he spoke, people listened because they knew that he kept a lot of opinions to himself. So when he did voice his sentiments, they were worthy of being heard.

Trey, wearing dark glasses, finally entered the quiet house. There was sun that day. He said, "Hello, Dad."

"Hello, son," Elisha responded as he put his coffee mug on the circular table.

"How was church?" Trey asked.

"Great, son. It's one of the best sermons I have ever heard." He paused and waited for Trey to sit down. When the silence remained too long, Elisha spoke up, "So, son, tell me, what brings you here? Of course I'm glad to see you, but I can tell when you have something heavy on your mind. What's going on?"

"Dad," Trey started as he got up and paced the floor as if to iron out his thoughts. "Flora's pregnant. So since I can't kill myself, I am getting married," Trey blurted out. He then sat down and removed the dark glasses revealing his bleary, baggy eyes.

"Trey," his father said calmly but sternly, "your attitude is wrong. How can you equate your wife-to-be with the notion of suicide?"

"Dad, she tried to kill herself because I was late calling her. I was in Atlanta attending a conference. I had to quit the conference. You know that dog, Hank, my coworker loved that. He had to read my work that I had agonized over for months. It was a grand opportunity for him to discredit me. It made me look awful in front of all my colleagues—"

"Calm down, Trey," Elisha cut in. "First, let me say that no man can harm you without your consent. Don't give these negative forces so much power in your life, and stop wondering about what others think. All people have shake-ups in their lives. As the saying goes, 'It's when you can say it's not so, you've overcome.'

"People may talk, but their challenges will be coming if they keep living. Compassionate people reach out to others in pain, not to find humor. Hopefully, you have been raised to be kinder and more compassionate, son.

"Your mother and I sacrificed a lot, but we mutually understood that your well-being came first. I feel that we did a good job on you, Trey. Where is your self-confidence? Your mother was extremely proud of you before she passed. However, there were more things that I would have liked to interject along the way. There are some things that only a man can tell a man becoming.

"Now listen. You're not the first person to get a woman pregnant, and I'm sure you won't be the last. That doesn't bother me in the least. An addition to the family could warm an old man's heart." He chuckled.

Elisha paused. He got up and picked up his coffee mug and his Bible. "Let's go to the kitchen. This is kitchen talk." Trey got up and followed his father into the kitchen. As his father fixed a fresh pot of coffee, he realized how much they actually looked alike. Trey could only hope to be that refined in his late sixties—if he lived that long, he thought. As they seated themselves with fresh mugs of coffee, they knew it was powwow time.

"Trey," Elisha resumed, "your feelings about Flora are very disturbing. How can you ever think of a good marriage when you're so hostile? Grant it, she does sound a bit deceitful, but we need to work on *your* emotions. I wanted to tell you more about men and their desires when you were in your preteens. Your mother strongly objected to my philosophy. She felt that there was no need for the discussion. Well, now is the time, I guess.

"I've always said to watch who you sleep with because they could get pregnant. Of course, you know I believe in giving the child your name. There is no compromise there. Sex for the mere pleasure of it is a dangerous game. A responsibility goes with it because people are involved, and they get hurt. I know you know this from seeing the aching people on the talk shows. You are old enough to really develop your spiritual life, and if you had been working on this a little harder, I doubt that you would have attracted Flora to you.

"Somewhere down the line, I know that there were some red flags that you ignored. You were into the flesh, son, and you missed some major warning signs. Marriage is no joke, and to marry someone you do not want to be with is like a sentence. I have seen a lot. In Romans 8:1, it says, 'There is therefore now no condemnation to them which are in Christ Jesus who walks not after the flesh but after the Spirit.' Trey, get out of this body syndrome. Come to the church with me. Continue to read your Bible. Each book is filled with timeless lessons. Does Flora have a church home?" he asked.

"No, Dad, she doesn't."

"Oh Lord. Well, we will work it out. This child must come here under the best possible circumstances. Illegitimacy is not an option in our family, Trey," he said, voice raised.

Trey knew that he had a lot to think about. He still had his room at his father's and knew that he was welcome to spend the night, but he felt that he needed to reflect on what he heard.

As he rose to leave, Elisha spoke softly. "Trey." He swallowed. "Pray, son. Pray for the strength to go through this."

"I will," he reassured his father.

"The child must have your name. God be with you," closed Elisha.

As Trey hugged Elisha for his wisdom and sound judgment, he breathed a little easier, and a certain peace enveloped him. He knew what he had to do, and he also knew that he had to raise his thinking to a more positive level. He had to take the lead in this affair and not be controlled by Flora's strong personality. He pulled his gray scarf tighter around his neck for strength and comfort as he backed out of the driveway with a smile. He felt more disciplined in his actions and knew that he had to first master his own emotions.

Chapter 17
Phoenix's Spiritual Order

aughing heartily, Phoenix wiped her mouth on her personalized napkin as she and her family sat around her mother's dinner table in Chicago. As she looked at the heights of her nephews and nieces, she realized that she had missed a lot. *Hard mission*, she thought to herself. She knew it would take some time to rejuvenate and come back together. But she quietly remembered the biblical promise, "I will restore to you the years the locusts have eaten."

She vowed that she would be patient with herself as she realized that she had given so much to others that she had exhausted herself. Yet her spiritual understanding reminded her that she saw her work there as successful. Her mind, body, and spirit would be replenished.

She attended a White Sox baseball game with her family and felt that the beautiful fireworks were expressly for her. She personalized each one with a *happy birthday*. "Home," she had once written, "where her mother's understanding awaited her. Home—where love was easy, simple, and pure."

After the celebration ended, more urgent callings set in as she knew that she needed to reestablish herself. Phoenix revisited her basic church home and leaned on that foundation quite heavily as she regained her direction. Great sermons and teaching helped assist her, and she started seeing good results in her life.

One day, Phoenix got a call from one of the places she had applied during her work search. It was a library, again, but the atmosphere was totally different, and the structure was brand a new. She felt honored to be chosen and readily accepted the offer as a young-adult librarian.

There was so much to learn, and this was just what she needed as she continually washed off the debris of the past. "New beginnings are blessings," she later wrote. As Ernest Holmes said in essence in *The Science of Mind* textbook, "It takes one drop of water at a time to clear a muddy pool."

She grew comfortable in her position and got an apartment in the building next door to her mother's. Her view from her living room was spacious and overlooked a lot of land. It allowed her to breath as new life continued to offer up rewards. Her aunt helped her buy a newer car so she could make the drives into the inner city to help her.

At her new job, one coworker gave her a grand compliment. She said, "Phoenix, you are so conscientious. You work with something until you get it in perfect order." She was referring to some of the book displays, graphic flyers, and bibliographies that Phoenix had created. Phoenix thanked her and knew within herself that this was a step-by-step process. Others felt that she was doing an outstanding job. She thought of Benjamin Franklin's quote, "Well done is better than well said."

Her biggest concerns were performing well on the job, decorating her new place, and helping her elderly aunt get out of the hands of the city's con artists. They had come to her under the guises of insurance agent, doctor, domestic help, and even spiritual advisor, all with the intent of swindling cash from her.

Her Aunt Louise had been in the same building for over thirty years, but things were changing, and this project was not an easy feat. No one handed Phoenix a *how-to* book, so she knew that she had to lean on her inner guide to show her how to accomplish this task.

First, she had to gain her aunt's confidence in the handling of her financial affairs. After this was achieved, she started looking for assisted-living places out in the southern suburbs close to where she lived. She wanted her close so she could check on her regularly. So her time was spent excelling on her job as well as gathering information on how to get her aunt into a safe and clean facility.

Each night in her empty apartment, Phoenix prayed for guidance and strength. She was fortunate enough to have found a second-hand furniture shop across the street where she picked up items on a regular basis. She knew she'd get back south to get her things and would later decide what she wanted to keep and what she would discard.

Phoenix got on her knees on a light-green mat and prayed for spiritual law and divine order. She kept a high watch regarding the desire for beer, and it seemed to be working because her life was happier. She had made the mental and physical sacrifice, and her blessings were abounding.

She successfully found a temporary assisted-living for her aunt and had her transported. The monthly costs were astronomical, and she knew that this could only last for a while. But her aunt, who was slipping into dementia, loved the beautiful surroundings, and she and her new roommate reminded Phoenix of first graders. They loved each other, and they sometimes held hands through this new adventure.

Phoenix had reunited with her childhood friend, and on one very cold Saturday, they met at her Aunt Louise's place. The movers had taken out the furniture and shipped it to another relative, and they cleaned out the apartment. Her aunt had so many new and untouched items from Marshall Field's, so they ended up giving the receptive neighbors on that floor many expensive gifts.

A lot of people were made happy, and they left the apartment with bounty and joy knowing that they had done the right thing. They followed in childlike innocence as they helped her father's only sister also embark on a higher and better life outside of the throes of the inner city.

Chapter 18
Trey's Spiritual Order

Trey changed his mind-set and tried to be optimistic as he supported Flora's ideas for wedding plans. He truly tried to lean on the spiritual side as he took full responsibility for his part in this outcome. However, he did not feel joyful as Flora left the hospital with a wedding list of about twenty people.

It dawned on him that she wasn't purposely keeping the list small. She just had a minimal number of friends, and the family was obligated to attend.

The wedding day was rainy and the atmosphere was drab. No one seemed really happy except Flora. Perhaps it was too soon after the hospital scare, and everyone could see that this was a tense situation.

Trey tried his best to grin through it, but Elisha could see the anguish in his son's eyes. It hurt the old man's soul, and he wondered if his own karma was trickling down to his only boy. He sat as still as a rock through the ceremony, and everyone seemed to be waiting the event to end.

Somehow, they stumbled through that September Saturday and landed into a bleak honeymoon in a downtown hotel. All Trey could see were the pills the doctors lined up on the hotel dresser and wondered how she could be in any shape to deliver and raise a child.

The words "as long as you both shall live" seemed to further tighten the tie around his neck. It was so final, and he wondered if he would ever feel really happy again. In the hotel room, he found a light jazz station to lighten the mood. He looked out over the usually blue

Lake Michigan, but today, it looked gray and choppy. Even the waters seemed disturbed. He caught a vague view of the John Hancock and the Prudential—a heavy fog engulfed them, preventing a clear view.

He thought about all the times he had taught symbolism in his literature classes. If he was reading the signs correctly, the road ahead looked bumpy and dreary. His shoulders sunk in a feeling of defeat because the only thing that the forecast did not predict was how long the ride would last. The voice behind him brought him back to the first lap of his marathon race.

"Trey, what are you thinking about?" Flora asked. To him, this was the most invasive, uncouth question any human being could ask another person.

"Nothing," he said flatly.

"Everybody thinks about something?" she probed.

"Flora, please. I just need some quiet time," he said coolly.

"Quiet time, quiet time. You're always squawking about quiet time," she quibbled. "What about me? I want you to hold me. I feel lonely and somewhat afraid."

"Afraid of what, Flora?" he asked.

"I'm afraid of being pregnant. I'm afraid I won't make a good mother. I'm afraid you don't love me enough," she continued.

And he thought, *I'm afraid I might lose my mind.* He said, "Come here." He sat down in the easy chair. She sat on his lap, curled upon his chest like a three-year-old. He held her, and he held his breath. She began to cry softly, and his soul screamed and raged with immense tears of pain and betrayal. But by all appearances, here was the strong, newlywed husband comforting his trembling new wife.

She went to sleep in his arms, and he finally eased her on to the bed and covered her with a blanket. She had said that the pills made her sleepy, and the music was getting on her nerves. So consummation was out.

"Too late for that anyway," he tried to joke to himself. He poured a glass of their celebration champagne and sat alone looking out of the window. He quietly enjoyed the beautiful lights of the Chicago skyline and refilled his glass until darkness loomed all around him. The lights gave him a vicarious thrill, an escape from his real and present dilemma.

"So this is my wedding day, and there lies my bride. Lord, I should have prayed more, I should have been more careful for sure. I should have . . . I should have . . . I should have . . ." Finally, he fell into a deep, intoxicated sleep in the chair.

He dreamt of his dream woman. She was attractive and smart, spirited, and someone who understood him and his line of work. He woke up and reality set in when he looked over and saw who was in the room with him. As the saying goes, "What goes around comes around." He was being candid and knew that he had to learn the lesson that this experience was teaching him.

He got up and joined Flora in bed, and it sounded like she was whimpering in her sleep as one does after a hard crying spell. He did not know what to do to make her happy or if he could make her happy. He adjusted the pillow under his head and remembered that he should take this time to pray while she was not observing him. He slid quietly out of bed and got on his knees on the light-green carpet. He asked God for patience and perseverance while he tried to guide himself and his new wife on a higher and elevated path.

Chapter 19

Phoenix's Zeal

Phoenix's zest for living was apparent to all who came in contact with her. Her efforts were paying off, and the youth at the library, her staff members, and certainly her family enjoyed being in her presence. Others felt her enthusiasm, and it spilled over to them in a positive way. The rippling laughter and sunny disposition, which were true to her nature, was revived as if it had been waiting for resurgence.

The library where she worked had high windows that emitted great light, and it added to her energy levels. When the automatic shades were opened, everyone's mood seemed to improve for the better. Even the seniors who came in early in the morning were more responsive and joy-filled when the blinds were opened.

"Good lighting brings real hope," she had written down. This bright library was also one of the first branches to have a drive-up window to either return or pick up books. This was an added feature to a lovely structure that housed a great collection as well. To add to the library's ambience, there was a large meeting room with a huge screen for viewing movies and giving presentations.

The large upstairs space was sometimes used for special events such as book sales. It was obvious to all who entered that a lot of time and dollars had been spent here, and they did not mind sharing their bounty. They had sent Phoenix and her colleagues to several local conferences to upgrade their skills and associations. This made her feel valued as a youth librarian, and she felt that she was evolving.

One particular morning, Phoenix felt extremely serene as she created a bibliography at her desk. The seniors sat around enjoying the morning newspapers and reading because the children were still in school. Her head was down when she heard a voice say, "Excuse me. Can you help me find some information on the Quakers?"

"Sure," Phoenix answered, not looking up until she had found a stopping place and flagged it. When she finally looked up, there stood a handsome, intelligent-looking man. His eyes showed levels of deep thought.

Have mercy! she thought to herself. She quickly smiled, packed her personal thoughts away, and put on the librarian look. She said, "Follow me." She assumed that he had come over to her because she was the only visible person at a desk.

As he followed her to the 800s section, Phoenix noticed how smooth and refined he was. She asked what exactly he was looking for, and he explained that he had to do a literary presentation on the Quakers' philosophy and spirituality. She started spewing out information on their persecution because of their beliefs in each person's individual light. She went on to mention how their beliefs intimidated others. He just stood there entertained by this animated delivery.

She realized she was talking too much and said, "Forgive me. Here are some books." She loaded up his arms.

"No, I love it," he replied. "Any specific writers in mind?"

"Yes. Try either John Woolman or John Greenleaf Whittier. In fact, try both. You'll see that, in a sense, they ran a relay race," she closed. "Good luck."

She returned to creating her list of books but smiled a secret smile and breathed. *It sure is refreshing to meet a fine and intelligent man. Too bad I didn't get a chance to check out that left ring finger."* She chuckled to herself.

His mere presence gave her a sense of hope that, just maybe, she might meet someone who made sense one day. *I could use those types of magical vibrations in my life,* she thought.

She was interrupted by the entrance of the wild afternoon scene— the children coming in at a zillion miles a minute. Unfortunately, she did not get a chance to see when he left, but he was etched deeply in her memory. She wore an unusually big smile, and coworkers and patrons commented on how radiant she seemed that day. It was a very good day, and she drove home feeling optimistic.

When she got home, she enjoyed the silence and just sat in quiet reflection for a while. She looked over at her bookshelf, got up, pulled out one of her literary anthologies, and got a bottle of water from the refrigerator. She eased down in her favorite burnt-orange chair and turned to Ralph Waldo Emerson's *Self-Reliance.*

She browsed through the essay and found a portion that she could not resist writing down. She copied, "It is easy in the world to live after the world's opinion; it is easy in solitude to live after our own." Her confidence was growing because her need for the approval of others was decreasing. She had stopped giving so much of her energy to others and was focusing on her own wholeness and well-being. And maybe, just maybe, she would be open to trying love again!

Chapter 20
Trey's Lack of Zeal

"Where have you been?" Flora snarled the minute she heard Trey close the door to their apartment.

"Just to the library, Flora," Trey answered.

"It does not take that long to go to the library. It's only ten minutes from here," she retorted.

"Well, it took longer because I went a very long distance to a very special one with an extensive literary collection. I get so sick and tired of you nagging and bitching the minute I reach the door. You almost made me lose my job. First, that death-scare shit when I was down at the conference in Atlanta. Then you gave Sandy an asthma attack with your surprise attack. She could have sued us! Now back off, Flora, damn it. It's been four months, and you make me not want to come home. Leave me alone before I continue and say things I can't take back. Now back off!" he said, raising his voice.

This was the way of the newlyweds. She had moved into his place, and he did not seem to adjust that well. Nothing of hers matched his. She seemed to abuse his items and take excellent care of her own. The house was often in disarray, but he recalled how well she kept her place.

They both stayed in bad moods. The cooking did not taste good anymore, and the lovemaking was loveless. Life in general was difficult. He dreaded going home, and he often stayed at work overtime to grade papers in a peaceful environment. When possible, he found other places to go to shorten the time that he had to be in her company.

At least during the dating period, she held back on some of these assaults. But now, it was a raw scene, and whatever came up in her mind, she let it roll out of her lips. She stayed angry perhaps because she knew deep inside that she was being tolerated and not fully loved.

He stormed into the bathroom and slammed the door and said, "It's too much!" He undressed for a shower. He got in, and as the warm water hit his back, he had another revelation. He thought, *Flora hasn't been gaining weight. I know I haven't been that attentive and am not quite sure what to look for, but something feels wrong here. It has been in the back of my mind, but every time I want to ask her questions about the pregnancy, she changes the subject.*

As the water relaxed his tense muscles, he hoped that this unproven revelation was something he could handle. The other issues surfaced as well. He found that he had become more profane with her, which he did not like, and his relationships with his colleagues had become more strained. He noticed that they were more distant since he had married Flora.

They knew about the Sandy incident, and they were just uncomfortable around her. He did not get invited to some of the functions he had once attended. His coworkers did not know how to handle her. That simple.

The more the water rolled off his body, the more at ease he began to feel. His mind began to clear slowly. He disliked confrontations, but he did not like to be agitated or accused unnecessarily. He had to get to the truth, and he also felt that he had to save himself. He had tried so many different ways to communicate with her and to entertain her, and very little seemed to be enough. At this point, he felt compelled to see what was really going on.

He turned off the shower, stepped out, and reached for a clean towel. He dried off slowly, and with each rub, his courage and quiet inner storm grew. He could no longer repress the need to express his concerns.

He reached and opened the door to exit the bathroom, and she lunged from behind the door and started yelling, "Where did these come from? How dare you keep these old love letters from that bitch? I've read every one of them. How dare you?"

"How dare *you*!" he hollered. "How dare you call her a bitch? You don't even know her. And how dare you read my mail! How dare you go searching through my things? Have you lost your damn mind? And by the way, are you really pregnant? Or was this just another crazy-assed stunt to mess up my life and make me pay for knowing you?"

He almost ran to the mirror to see where this bellowing sound was coming from. He couldn't believe that he had lost control like this. When he did catch a glimpse of himself in the mirror, he saw a neurotic, naked man shaking like a leaf. He knew then that this was the end of the road. He had just crossed over into insanity.

Flora stood there with her mouth open. She had never seen him like this before. First, she was speechless. Her untiringly scheming mind was caught off guard for a minute. Then she tried tears; they wouldn't come as quickly as usual. So she feigned affection and saw that he seemed to be made of marble. Finally, she just sat down and started fidgeting with the upholstery in his favorite chair. Then she started to chip the nail polish from her fingers.

This time, he had seen it all and was not fooled by her antics. He quietly took out a set of sheets and an orange comforter and said affirmatively, "I'll be sleeping on the couch tonight." He made up the couch with no enthusiasm. He felt drained and depleted.

Trey could see one lesson that he had learned already. Some people could make you laugh and feel light, and some people could bring out the darkest traits. He tried to muster the strength to pray, but he doubted if he could be heard because his spirit was so broken from the war.

He lay down quietly as he heard Flora starting up a crying spell. He slowly got up and closed the door between them. He felt that he had seen and heard it all. If he had been wrong about questioning the validity of a pregnancy, he would promptly admit it. Time would tell all because babies were not illusive.

Eventually, like a tired warrior, he was lulled into a deep sleep. Strangely enough, in a flash, the librarian with the beautiful smile whom he had met earlier that day seemed to be standing over him. "What a delight," he muttered audibly. This vision was a welcome anecdote to his current riveting drama, and it offered him hope that better things lay ahead.

Chapter 21

Phoenix's Renunciation

Phoenix woke up and smiled when she realized that she had the day off in the middle of the week. She felt a sense of freedom and sat until she could clearly see how she would spend this day. She looked out and noticed that the sun was shining brightly, and the conditions were dry. "Maybe I'll drive down to the lake and let the breeze clear my mind." She smiled.

After coffee, journaling, and the reading of her spiritual perks, Phoenix decided that the lake was calling her name. She was obedient and strongly felt that it was the right course of action. Seeing the beautiful Lake Michigan was always a delight, especially for those who did not get to see it on a regular basis.

She felt nudges to head in that direction as she listened to the cawing of birds and saw the brightly shining sun. She prepared to go after getting herself together. She grabbed her russet windbreaker and a white scarf on her way out of the apartment.

Phoenix drove north and listened to good music on the radio. She had planned to go to the Fifty-Seventh Street Beach where she had historical ties. But when she got there, she could not find parking. After feeling a little frustrated, she knew that she was not where she needed to be at that time. She let the car idle for a while in the full parking lot and silently listened for instructions. She let go of the original plan and got back on the drive and continually headed north.

Traffic became backed up north of McCormick Place, and after getting in the right lane, she chose to exit right at the Museum

Campus exit. She found parking with ease and said, "Have it your way, Lord." She parked and got her books, magazines, and a blanket out of the car. She hummed as she headed toward the water. She did not want to go in the museums that day, but she did want to enjoy the outdoors.

Phoenix walked along the path close to the water and enjoyed the wind as her mind cleared. She knew that this was the divine spot at that moment, so she stopped questioning and simply relaxed. She found a place to spread her blanket, and she pulled out some nuts and a bottle of water and flipped through one of her new magazines.

She enjoyed the immense beauty of the clear blue sky and the sailboats on the crystal blue water. She sat there for a while when she noticed a woman who was sitting uncomfortably close to the lake. She was perched on a rock, and her feet were dangling over toward the water. The news reported water rescues all the time of people who ended up in the water. This was an unsettling scene, and she did not want to be a witness to any tragedy.

Phoenix got up and walked over to her and gently said, "Hi." She did not want to startle this person. As the woman turned to see who was speaking, Phoenix immediately recognized her old college friend.

"Willow? How have you been, girl?" she asked, hoping to lighten the mood.

"Phoenix? Hey. I heard that you were back in Chicago," she responded.

"Yeah. I have been back for almost a year. Let's catch up. Why don't you come over and sit on my blanket over there? I have extra water and a huge bag of nuts to share," added Phoenix.

Willow took a moment and finally stood up. Phoenix took her hand and led her to the blanket like a child. When they both were seated, she offered Willow bottled water and poured a handful of mixed nuts in her hand. They sat for a while, and Phoenix started talking about some of the hardships she had had in the mid-south.

Willow seemed to be listening but still sat in a trance-like state. But Phoenix kept talking as if painting a canvas because it was all she had to try and bring this woman back from this grave-like state. Then, in a flash, Phoenix started talking about her disappointment in love and the betrayal she had experienced with her boyfriend and fair-weather friend, Lila.

At that moment, she saw a movement in Willow, and Phoenix knew that she had hit the spot. *The affairs of the heart. Always the rub,* she thought to herself. Willow started her yarn, and her hands moved as she told what had happened in her life. Phoenix sat quietly and relaxed because she did not want to do anything to stop Willow from getting it all out.

Willow spoke and told how she had met a guy whom she considered a real catch. He had more education than she did and had a high-powered job at a law firm in the Loop. She wanted to be all that he wanted in a woman, and she felt that things were coming along.

He had proposed, and she had started planning her wedding. But the past caught up with her, and one of her old boyfriends got in touch with her. She knew that he loved her but also knew that he did not have his life in order. He could whisper sweet nothings, but there was no way he could truly provide for her. He had children from two other women, and she felt that there would always be some conflict and confusion.

She had made the mistake of letting him come by her place. She planned to tell him all about her new plans and hoped that he loved her enough to let her go and wish her the best. However, things got heated and she fell back into his old net.

The doorbell rang, and when Willow answered it, a florist delivered a bouquet of roses. As she was signing for them, her new beau stood behind the delivery guy, smiling. She was totally caught off guard, and when he peered over her shoulder and saw that she had company, it was as if his face broke into a thousand pieces.

Willow started crying and Phoenix was glad that she had some tissues in her purse. *Nothing like being prepared,* she had thought. After the tears flowed for quite some time, Phoenix touched Willow softly and said, "It is good that you can talk and let this go. Life happens, and we do not always know why." She looked for the right words and thought of one of Emily Dickinson's lines that goes, "Saying nothing sometimes says the most."

Tears flowed from both of them, and Phoenix realized that she had not taken time to cry about her own pain. She had been so busy rebuilding her life that she had not looked into her own dark hole.

When they dried their tears, Phoenix said, "Sometimes a good cry can cleanse the soul. It is a way to repent and make us realize what we must give up in order to go forth. We have to renounce the old and gravitate toward the new." She was shocked at her own words and was not quite sure where the wisdom had come from.

"Willow? Have you spoken with him?" Phoenix asked.

"He won't talk to me. Some of the things he said were horrible. And of course, when the pressure came, the old flame disappeared," Willow added.

"Good," said Phoenix. "Hopefully, you can move on up a little higher. Did you drive?"

"No. I took the bus so I could think," Willow answered.

"Come on, and I will take you home. We can talk more on the way," Phoenix volunteered.

They both got up and brushed themselves off. They headed to Phoenix's car in a more relaxed state of mind, and after getting directions, she drove Willow to her place in the city.

When they reached Willow's place, they sat in the car and talked. "Let's pray for our right mates, Willow," said Phoenix. They held hands as Phoenix asked the universe to send them the right mates that could help them on their life journeys. They exchanged numbers and vowed to call and talk if things seemed too heavy to bear. Talking was better than giving up, they both had agreed.

They hugged each other, and as Willow ascended the stairs of her apartment, she looked less droopy, and there was light and hope in her eyes. She turned and waved at Phoenix, and her smile lit up the sky. Phoenix understood her mission for that day. She had been further washed and was glad to know that it had been in the company of a friend. They were both the better for the encounter, and that night, Phoenix slept very peacefully. She muttered, "I am moving forward slowly but surely."

Chapter 22
Trey's Renunciation

There surely was no smiling or laughter in Trey's and Flora's lives. The arguments grew, the respect waned, the name-calling ensued, and each day was a day of torment. Trey tried to practice his daily meditations, but they were usually interrupted by questions like "Why are you so quiet?" or "What are you reading?" Flora would say, "I can't stand the quiet. I have to have some noise, either some music or television." He stayed irritated, and it was adversely affecting his job performance because he could not concentrate.

He was often a few minutes late for his classes, and others detected either an aloofness or disorientation. One irritating student, usually found in every class, saw that he was off-center and found ways to agitate his soul during literary explanations. Trey was repeatedly challenged, and it took all he had to keep his composure and not lose control.

One day, he told the class to excuse him and the student. He took him outside and told him that if he couldn't listen, take notes, or stop heckling, he would be dropped from the class like a parachute from a speeding plane. That was the end of that problem. The student needed the class to graduate.

In his office, he looked at his plaque of the "Desiderata" and saw the line that read "noisy people are a vexation to the spirit." He nodded in agreement as he thought of Hank's sarcasm and constant digs and Flora's verbal attacks when he reached home. Trey didn't know how much longer he could endure this and said, "Something has got to give, Lord."

He and Flora had been waiting for almost three weeks for an appointment with a gynecologist. This time, he reconfirmed the appointment and wanted to hear what the doctor had to say. She always claimed that her fits of rage and crying were due to her hormonal imbalance. He privately questioned that because of the memories of horrid events before the pregnancy.

The day arrived, and he left work to pick up Flora. When he got home, she was sitting in his favorite chair in the dark with the curtains drawn. Her hair was in disarray, and she resembled a madwoman.

"Flora? Why aren't you ready?" he asked.

No answer.

"Flora? You know we have to be at the doctor's office in an hour. It's a twenty-minute drive."

Suddenly, she burst into tears and said, "I can't. I know you don't love me, and you don't want this baby. That's why you're checking behind me."

He decided not to respond but secretly felt like crying himself. He thought, *And she's going to raise a child?* "Flora, you have ten minutes to get dressed. My job is already on the line," said Trey.

"There you go blaming me for everything, Trey," she whined.

"You've got ten minutes to get it together or I'm filing for a divorce, Flora," screamed Trey. She left and started getting ready, but by then, Trey was visibly upset after having to go to this level to get her to cooperate.

Once they arrived at the doctor's office, and Flora had gone in to see the doctor, Trey flipped through the available magazines trying to regain his composure. They had screamed all the way to the doctor's office. There were more than enough accusations, blame, and personal attacks to spread around.

Flora came from the room looking bewildered and frightened. Trey said, "Flora, what is it?"

She just sat numbly, playing with her hands. She finally mumbled, "The doctor wants to speak with you." Then she started to cry.

"Flora, what is it? Get a hold of yourself. People are staring at us," he coaxed.

"Just go in and talk with the doctor. She's waiting for you," she said flatly. Trey nervously got up, and the receptionist led him into the doctor's office. Once in, he took a seat and waited for the doctor's arrival. After entering the office, she said, "Hello, I'm Dr. Gray. Your wife has a somewhat rare case of what we term pseudocyesis."

Trey just sat there still confused.

The doctor continued, "She has missed periods and had all of the symptoms of pregnancy such as morning sickness and nausea, but we could not find a heartbeat. In layman's terms, there is no baby. We strongly believe that the pregnancy was mentally induced, and this is a false pregnancy. It is a rarity in medicine, and we have done some studies on these cases.

"However, they are obviously psychological, and oftentimes, the mother has a strong need to have a maternal bond and attachment. They thereby go through several of the stages of an actual pregnancy, even gaining weight. But ultimately, the reality outweighs the psychological because no baby is ever born," she said.

Trey sat there stunned and speechless. He did not say a word. His head seemed to pound as the words touched his soul. He wondered how on earth he had drawn something like this into his life. He knew he was paying dues, but he wanted to shout "Lord, have mercy!" As he sat there appearing to be a composed and caring husband, he just looked ahead with a removed look in his eyes. There were no words.

When Dr. Gray saw that he had nothing to add or subtract, she continued and said, "I know this is hard for you and your wife. I'm sure you were looking forward to your little bundle of joy, but I have prescribed a sleep aid for her to ease her through the shock. Also, I have arranged visits for her with a family counselor as well. Do take good care of her and yourself. Here is a pamphlet that I downloaded on false pregnancy if you want to read more." "Thanks," Trey answered as he rose to leave. "Thank you, Dr. Gray, for the information," he closed as he remembered his manners. Trey gathered himself and his coat and quietly walked to the waiting room. Then he gathered Flora, and they left and went to their car. Once inside, the silence was like a morgue. No words, no music, just private thoughts.

Thoughts flourished.

Trey's thoughts: *Well, we can annul the marriage or get a divorce. I can start over. I'll start calling around for legal advice.*

Flora's thoughts: *Maybe I can calm the waters with Trey. Maybe I can really get pregnant this time. I can't take back all the things I have said and done, but I do want this marriage to work.*

Trey's thoughts: *Lord, if I can just ease out of this one, I promise I'll take my time before I jump in bed with a woman again. I'll take the time to check out her mind. I know that I brought this on myself by, as Dad said, being into the flesh. Please forgive me, Lord.*

Flora's thoughts: *After we get this prescription filled, I'll ask him to stop and get some champagne. I don't think I need the pills tonight, but it won't hurt to have them. I'll fix us a special dinner, put on some soft music, and get him in a mood to ease the stress. Oh, I don't want to lose him.*

Silence.

"Trey, can we stop by the store? I would like to get this prescription filled and get a couple of other items," Flora whined.

"What other items?" asked Trey.

"Champagne and nuts," she said.

"Why champagne, Flora? What are we celebrating?" he asked.

"Us. Our ability to get through this together," she answered.

Silence and private thoughts.

Trey's thoughts: *Maybe champagne is a good idea. If I get high enough, I can mention an annulment or a divorce.*

Flora's thoughts: *I can't give him too much time to think. I have to make this right.*

"Okay. Let's stop, but don't take too long. We both need to rest," said Trey.

Flora's thoughts: *Yeah, rest.*

Once they shopped and got home, silence loomed in the air as they both started to work on their plans.

"Flora," Trey started, "Couldn't you tell that something was wrong?"

"How could I know? I haven't had children before," she answered.

"How did you decide you were pregnant in the first place, Flora?"

"I had begun to miss periods," she responded.

"It could have been your nerves after the suicide attempt," he quibbled.

"Oh, you had to bring that up, didn't you?"

"It happened," he said.

Silence.

Flora decided to fix one of his favorite dishes. He, in turn, decided to relax and play the game so he could eventually lay his cards on the table as well. Both operated stealthily with their private thoughts and hidden agendas.

After eating the scrumptious meal Flora had prepared, they retired to the living room. Soft music played, and they sipped champagne quietly. Flora dabbed her eyes and pretended to cry softly. Deep within, she was determined to win again at any cost.

"Trey, do you think—" She stopped.

"What, Flora?" he answered softly.

"Do you think we could try again?" she continued.

"Try what? To make the relationship work? Now you know that—"

"For a baby," she cut in.

"A baby? A baby?" he exclaimed, his voice raised. "Flora, I don't want a baby, I want a divorce." He shocked himself with what he just said.

"A divorce? A divorce?" she screamed.

"Well, an annulment or whatever. You know and I know that this is not working. There is not a moment's peace when we're together. Either you're accusing me of every woman I walk by or bringing up old love affairs. You even read my old mail. I let you move into my place, and you roamed through my possessions before I could discard what I felt I no longer needed. But you didn't give me a chance.

"You keep me upset, and it has affected my work, my career, my metabolism, and my lack of spirituality. First, you took a bunch of pills, and now the pregnancy farce! And you expect me to like you? You're a walking hurricane, Flora. Everything in your path is destroyed and turned upside down like my life is right now. I promised my father I would do the right thing, but enough is enough. Since there is no baby coming and no peace in sight, I want *out*," he said emphatically.

He was now nervously pacing the floor as his words seemed to emit steam from his shivering body. He didn't like being pushed to this level, and she had a knack for pushing his buttons. Trey walked over and sat down when he realized that he was giving her power over his better judgment. He poured another glass of champagne and sat in his lounge chair by the window.

She came toward him and he said, "Stay away from me, Flora. This could get ugly, uglier than we need to experience. Stay back and let me have some quiet time."

"But, Trey, I can't believe you said those things to me," she said. "Please, Trey, please reconsider. What will people think?" she cried.

"People? What people? You have no friends. What people? I couldn't care less what people think. Most of them who pass an opinion have much more to hide than we do. Besides, you make me lose respect for you. You make me say things that I have to think about later and make me question myself. Let's quit this conversation before the words start flowing again, Flora. I have never talked to anyone like this before in my life," he said.

She stood over him for a moment. "Will you hold me, Trey, and tell me that everything will be all right?" she pleaded.

"No. No more pretenses. No more games, Flora. I need to be alone," he said.

"We could talk about this," she continued.

"I need to be alone," he said in a low, definitive voice.

"But, Trey?"

He did not answer.

"Trey?" she said.

He still did not answer her.

She walked over, refilled her glass of champagne, went into the bedroom, and closed the door. He poured glass after glass as he sat in the lounge by the window, sinking deeper and deeper into self-pity and depression. Sleep finally overtook him as he admitted to himself that he had brought on these unhappy conditions through his overindulgence and lack of discernment.

The birds were chirping loudly as he woke up and saw that he had actually slept in the chair. His back hurt, and he said, "Oh, my aching head!" He looked at the clock and saw that he had overslept and would be late for work.

"Oh Lord, I have to call the job and tell them something. Oh, oh, oh . . ." He stood and held his heavy head. He gained his stance and realized that Flora was not up either. He opened the door to the bedroom and saw that she was still sleeping. "Humph."

He went into the bathroom to rejuvenate himself. As he was washing his face, a revelation hit him. He thought, *She's mighty still.* He quickly walked over. He saw how motionless she lay there.

"Flora?" he shook her gently.

No response. An empty bottle of the prescribed pills fell to the floor.

"Oh God!" he screamed. "Oh my god. Lord, help me please! Oh God." He was shaking. After remembering to call 911, he did so as he paced the floor like a robot. The only words that would come out were "Oh God."

After the paramedics arrived with the unforgettable flashing russet lights and all business was taken care of, he did finally call his job. He found an excuse for not reporting after all. He told the department secretary, "I will not be in today. My wife is *dead.*" He was able to pronounce the word.

Trey felt numb, empty, and confused. He had lost a wife and the prospect of a child in less than twenty-four hours. He felt lost as he asked for divine instruction. How on earth was he going to live through this? Would the guilt consume him? He knew he could not fool God, and he knew that this ordeal would not be easy to live down. In a meek and childlike fashion, he walked over to the phone and called his father.

Chapter 23

Phoenix's Life

Phoenix became increasingly aware of her improved health and overall state of mind. She gave more attention to her own needs, which may have appeared as selfishness to some, but she knew it was required to retune and refine her own life.

She was glad for the reunion with Willow and hoped that she said something that had helped her on that day at the lakefront. She admitted that she needed the connection as much as Willow did and now understood why she was led to that location on that day. "There is strength in numbers," she breathed.

Her battle scars were slowly healing, and she returned home as a much stronger warrior than the "love me" type that had left years before. J. Herbert Brewster, a songwriter, wrote the song "Be Proud of Your Wounds and Scars," and Phoenix was proud of her newfound life and vowed to hold out in the affairs of the heart until she could attract one who knew his own spiritual center. No compromise there.

She had squandered her life energy by dealing with the physical, and now she would take up problems from the spiritual standpoint. It seemed simple, but Phoenix now understood that the stakes were too high when involved with a spiritually depraved person.

"No more," she resolved. She became more resilient, and her sweetness and purity reemerged. She and her mother, Septima, were very close, and they spent hours talking about the books that they shared. When she shared some of her experiences with one of her cousins, she had said, "You? Not you." She had seen these failings as inconceivable, and it helped put Phoenix back on track.

She became much more cautious when choosing her associations and was seen by some as a loner. She looked up at a quote that she had painted and put on a piece of stretched canvas. "Associate yourself with men of great quality if you esteem your own reputation for 'tis better to be alone than in bad company," George Washington had said.

A whole year had passed. The job was fine. The place was fine. She had gotten her furniture from the south. Everything was fine except now she decided one thing was missing from her life. Her soul mate. She had made herself content, but she felt that it was time—or at least she could ask and see if her timing was right.

As a form of therapy, she picked up her ever-ready legal pad and pen and formulated her thoughts. First, she just sat still for a while. Then the pen started moving from left to right across the page. "Two hearts," she started. "Two hearts joined by one horizontal string," she continued. "And when there is a weight placed on that string, and the tension on the line increases. That can be equated with pain or even cause screams. Or when that string is free to keep both hearts equally balanced, the harmony of the notes vibrates as on a lute or a violin," she closed.

She said, "Lord, it is time." She decided to have a ritualistic sacred night. First, she bathed in the silence by candlelight. She quietly meditated with no particular thoughts. No crosscurrents. No thoughts moving like speeding bullets. Just calm, pensive thoughts.

"Pensive thoughts, pensive moods, ease the friction of the mind," she had formerly written. She quietly repeated this until, while still in the tub, she could feel a deep trance-like state engulfing her. She closed her eyes, saw rainbows flashing before her eyes, and relaxed deeply.

After a couple hours of soaking and constantly reheating the water, Phoenix got out of the tub. She took olive oil and anointed her head and her feet, asking for understanding, protection, and guidance. She took the candle and placed it high enough to be seen.

She kneeled down on a clean red towel she had spread on the bathroom floor and prayed, "Lord. I need your help. I come to you as your humble child. I know you know what is best for me. I have run this race as long as I can alone, Lord. I need my help mate. I have no problems serving you and being your hands here on earth. But Lord, I could do so much more, be so much more, and achieve so much more if I had my mate by my side. I am tired doing it all alone. I will not tell you how he should look, Lord, because I trust you to answer the call.

"My minister told me not to overstate the case, Lord, so I will not go on and on. But I must add one thing. He absolutely must have his spiritual life straight. He must have a fear of you as well and must also be seeking his mate. I am finished with nonbelievers in my life, world, and affairs. I ask this in your name and in the name of the Father, the Son and the Holy Spirit. Amen and amen."

She got up, put on some red silk pajamas, and crawled quietly into bed. She felt relaxed and illumined. She had a spiritual awakening as the result of the many steps she had taken. She vowed to carry the message to others and to continue to practice the principles in all affairs. She thanked God for his divine protection. She remembered a quote from Frederick Douglass which said that "power concedes nothing without a demand." She had paid the price.

When sleep did not immediately come, she turned on the light, and picked up her pad and pen. She wrote,

In Twos

All of nature travels in glorious twos;
With perfect pairing, you can't lose.
Geese fly together to observe below,
Realizing the reaping they can sow.
One may fall from apparent sight,
The other rescues with all its might.
Silent communication or chattering in which
Each has an anchor to lasso or hitch.
It is a blessing when likes magnetically attract
Someone special to always have your back.

She read over her verse and said, "It is a little rough, but the universe understands. She turned off the light and let the words soar toward the all-knowing heavens.

Chapter 24
Trey's Life

Trey's life showed glimmers of hope as he moved forward after Flora's funeral. He had grieved deeply and some seemed surprised by how hard he had cried. Onlookers did not understand that grieving was an opportunity to cry for what was and what should have been. He grieved for the fact that she had never learned to love herself. She was named for a flower, just one that never fully bloomed and did not reach its potential beauty.

He grieved deeply for himself as well. He knew he would have feelings of guilt for a long time to come. He grieved for the lack of understanding they never achieved, and he grieved because he was a widower at such a young age. She had definitely left her mark on his life. He finally realized that she was there to help him grow and get very serious about his choices in women and in life itself.

His father, Elisha, had been most supportive during this challenging time. They had grown closer than ever. Even Hank had become more humane, as people often do in the midst of a crisis. The year had been dampened with tears and multiple emotions. But through it all, the outstretched arms of his father, coworkers, and ever-loving students had helped him to survive. He then decided it was time to thrive, to *be*.

After a year had passed, at others' insistence, he tried a few blind dates. Nothing truly clicked, and he knew that the fog of the marriage had not truly lifted. He did like the concept of marriage and knew that it brought protection, purity, and soul communion. But he would take his time.

He could *breathe again*. He turned on the radio and heard Frankie Beverly and Maze's "Golden Time of Day." He smiled faintly and relaxed. It had been a difficult year, but taking one day at a time, he had made it through to the finish line.

Trey spent more weekends at his father's, and the rides out to the south suburbs was also a way to continually get the cobwebs released from his mind. They attended church together, and on occasion, he went with his father to bowl.

He kept himself equipped with positive literature and CDs to listen to as he drove. He knew what careless thinking can draw into one's life, and he did not feel he could survive another onslaught of being with misguided or unenlightened people. As he read Mary Baker Eddy's *Science and Health*, she reminded her readers to "stand porter at the door of thought."

The thought of companionship crept briefly into his mind, but he quickly washed it out as he cleaned the bathtub. He felt that a bath instead of a shower would help him make friends with water and embrace the idea of wholeness.

This tub was not as lavishly built as the one in his former apartment. After Flora's overdose, he had moved to work on regenerating his own life. He added bath salts and bubble bath to increase the invitation to a holy wash. He would appeal to the gods and ask for repentance and instruction.

Trey eased into the tub, relaxed, and closed his eyes. First he thought, *Tyre, my real name, means "rock." Dad says by using my nickname of Trey, I am not living to my true potential because I am not calling forth the true idea meant for me. He said I need to be steady like a rock and that Tyre was an ancient island known for its artistic craftsmanship and shipbuilding. There were traders of purple dyes. Purple means power in itself. Tyre means rock.* "I want to be strong and as steady as a rock. I want to exude power," he spoke aloud.

"Tyre. Humph," he tried out his given name. Silence. "Lord, I am ready for my good. I want a good woman in my life. No, I want a wife. I want someone that will be here for me every day, day in and day out. I want her to have a career of her own though, Lord. I want her to have her own goals in life. Perhaps we can help each other realize our personal dreams. I want us to operate as a unit, but as Kahlil Gibran says in *The Prophet*, 'Let there be spaces in your togetherness.'

"And, oh, Lord, please let her have a love for reading and the printed word. It is a necessity to counteract and balance what I do for a living. Let her have clean, wholesome morals, and please let her love herself, which means she'll know how to love me. I won't tell you how she should look. I'll trust you to know what will complement me.

"Oh yes, Lord." He paused. "She absolutely must believe in you." He silently recalled a quote from 2 Corinthians 6:14 that his father had him write down. "Be ye not unequally yoked together with unbelievers: for what fellowship hath righteousness with unrighteousness and what communion hath light with darkness?"

He turned on the hot water to warm the bathwater, leaned out, and picked up a towel. He got out and dried off and wrapped it around him. He kneeled down on the red rug and said, "Forgive me, Most Reverent One. I come before you again as I humbly state my case." He started all over again now that he was in the right position to beseech his Father's help.

Afterward, he kept his eyes closed and saw colors, sparkles, and scintillating lights. The color gold flashed. He opened his eyes and smiled, "Yes. She will be a piece of gold." He knew that she had to be virtuous like the woman described in Proverb 12:4. As his father had read, "She's a crown to her husband." *Lord, I could use a crown,* he thought.

Tyre rose and put on a pair of new pinstriped pajamas. The feel of the new cotton against his skin signaled the new blessings that would flow his way. Using his given name, he felt more confident that his name was written in heaven. That thought brought a smile to his face as he lay down. He felt sure that it was only a matter of time before his prayers were answered.

Chapter 25

Consummation

The crows were cawing. Another sunny day. Phoenix smiled as she opened her eyes. *Yes! It truly helps my spirits.* She thought about the true meaning of the phoenix bird after which she was named. "I feel rejuvenated, renewed. I can safely say I have turned over several new leaves," she affirmed.

Phoenix recalled the Native American writer who taught the audience how to say, "Out of ashes, peace will rise." They had to say it as they faced all directions. She carried out the ritual with her hands in the air, laughing lightly at herself. She was glad that she was not being observed and again gave thanks that it was a Saturday and a day of *no work*.

No work. Praise God, Tyre thought as he awakened. He readjusted his pillow. He could see that it was sunny day and decided on the lakefront. "I am ready for something fresh, new, and wonderful. The water always reminds me that life is continuous," he said as his feet hit the floor.

Balancing herself from her ritual, Phoenix brewed some coffee, pulled out her daily meditations, and sat in the silence as she read and pondered messages. She breathed deeply and pulled in thoughts of new beginnings. Every time her mind wanted to pull her back into troubled waters, she resolved to keep swimming.

Speaking of swimming, she thought. *I think I would like to see the lake. Nothing is as refreshing as that beautiful blue water that charges the mind with imagination and miles and miles of immense possibilities. Yes, the lake is for me. Think I will go early while the day is freshly painted, while the newness of the Spirit is still on the earth and most of the freaks are still sleep.* She chuckled.

"All right, Tyre. Tyre. Tyre. Sounds okay, even to me. No more sleep. Do your meditation and get out and enjoy this morning sacredness. Remember, Franklin said that 'the early bird catches the worm,'" he spoke aloud.

He clicked on the coffeepot, walked over to open the blinds to emit the dawning sun, and noticed the prism of colors that his suspended crystal reflected on the wall. *Oh yes. This doesn't happen often. It's going to be a special day. Rainbows are blessings, they say. And you have to be in the right place at the right time to catch them. They don't last long, but seeing one is a memory etched in the mind for a lifetime,* he thought.

After spending some quiet time in communion, Tyre eased from his favorite chair. Slowly, almost methodically, he walked to the bathroom. He moved very quietly as he took off his pajamas and got into the shower. He put his head under the falling water, and it felt as though he was being baptized, cleansed, and spiritualized. He moved just as peacefully from the shower and felt renewed. He dried off and walked to the bedroom with peace in every step.

He quietly put on his jeans, a yellow cotton top, his jacket, socks, and gym shoes. He picked up the keys to his car, some daily meditation guides, and some of his favorite music. He made sure all the appliances were off, then he closed the door to his apartment and locked it. He wasn't sure of his exact destination but asked for the wisdom to be led to wherever the Spirit was pulling him.

Pulling on her gold sweater over her head, Phoenix moved rapidly as though there was some urgency. She threw on some skinny jeans, grabbed a mug of coffee, took a few CDs, and headed for the stairs. She had checked everything in her house as a safety precaution before leaving. After buckling her seat belt, she started on her journey.

She deeply said, "I know you'll give me understanding as to these callings." The birds were cawing incessantly as though beckoning her onward. She drove north toward the beach. "Think I'll try Fifty-Seventh Street beach. That's where our family started out. It has good karma for me. She drove like a robot, as though everything was predestined. Then she heard two versions of the song "I'll Be There." First it was by Michael Jackson and then by Mariah Carey. She relaxed and breathed out. "Not my will but thine be done."

As if by some force, Tyre was being pulled in the southern direction. He drove with ease as if the car was being cosmically guided. Traffic was sparse, and everything seemed to be wide open. "Which beach?" he asked for direction. "Which beach should I go to?" he said out loud. He first saw a sign saying Interstate 57.

"Okay. If I see it again, I'll know that it'll be Fifty-Seventh Street Beach." Before completing that statement, a car zoomed by with its emergency flashers. Its license tags were PT5757. "Okay. It's resolved. Fifty-Seventh Street beach, here I come." When Stevie Wonder's song "Ribbon in the Sky" came on, he relaxed and stated, "Have your way with me, Lord."

Upon arriving, he found parking on Fifty-Sixth Street. *Lucky me,* he thought. He breathed in the fresh air, pulled out a deep-blue scarf from the back of the car for good measure, wrapped it around his neck, and started walking toward the pedestrian overpass. The walk was good and brisk, and it cleared his mind. Once over the overpass, he found a rock and sat down.

He said to himself, "Think I'll sit here sideways facing the south so I can catch most of the four directions. This is nice, but it's still the city." He sat quietly on the rock of his choice and "waited" for understanding. He enjoyed the sky, the moving clouds, the beautiful sun, the cool breeze, and the birds flying in formation. The joggers passed by, and other people walked at different paces.

Phoenix found parking on Fifty-Sixth Street. She felt fortunate because parking was difficult to find in the Hyde Park area. She bundled up, zipped up her jacket, and reached in the back of the seat for her gold scarf. "Lucky me," she said, "I match today." She closed the car door, crossed the street silently, and started up the stairs to the pedestrian overpass as she chanted the Prayer of Protection. Once on the walkway, she pranced. "I go to meet my good." She descended the stairs dramatically with the grace of a swan, not realizing that she was being observed.

Tyre looked at her and said, "Hmm. Gold. True gold on gold."

She looked around once she reached flat land. She saw a man sitting sideways on a rock and said, "Oh, God, not this morning, please." So she bypassed him and went a bit farther and found a rock on which to rest.

As she passed, Tyre thought, *That looks like the librarian from Homewood Library. This is deep. The one who shared information about Woolman and Whittier.*

"I hope he doesn't come over her trying to rap, Lord. I came for peace and privacy," Phoenix muttered.

He waited until she had settled herself on her chosen rock. He bided his time and gave her time to breathe. He timed his moves and approached cautiously. "I know you probably want your privacy, but don't you work at the Homewood Library?" Tyre asked after he got his nerves up to approach her.

"Yes," she retorted until she looked around into his face. "Oh yes." She softened when their eyes met. "I remember you."

"Quakers?" he added.

"Yes, for your research." Phoenix affirmed.

"Yes. So you came to enjoy the pool of silence and drop your burdens?" asked Tyre.

"Yes," she said.

"Me too," he said. "Can I sit with you?"

"Sure," she responded, feeling a sense of safety. "They say there is strength in numbers."

"By the way, my name is Tyre. It means rock, though I've gone by a nickname for years."

"I am Phoenix. It represents daily renewal like the phoenix bird."

"Okay." He smiled, revealing one dimple on the left cheek.

Silence.

"I am a recent widower with no children," volunteered Tyre.

"I am a lot of things with no children." Phoenix laughed.

"Single?" he asked.

"Yes," she responded.

Yes, gold, he thought to himself. He peered up into the heavens and smiled his thanks. The words "Gold and crown to her husband" rolled around in his mind.

She remembered some lines from an Emily Dickinson poem she'd learned in college.

With Will to choose, or to reject,
And I choose, just a Crown.

She looked up into the sky and thought to herself, *Yes, out of ashes, peace will rise.*

Silence.

They rested just as musical compositions take rests. After fighting a raging war, they were two people tugging against dark forces in an effort to retrieve the other halves of their souls.

They sat in the silence and listened to the waves hit against the rocks. After a long silence, they turned to each other, searched out each other's eyes, the windows to the soul, and said warmly and in unison, "Hi."

They invited each other in. They both understood what had just occurred. Their hearts twinkled silently because they knew that their faith had brought them through the storms and brought about answered prayers. They had found the ultimate gift—love.

Love is pink, soft, and true,
And erases any feeling of blue.
Love is round and spongy too,
'Cause it bounces back on you.
Love is colorful and bright
And fills the soul with delight.

Phoenix was inspired to write this when she returned home. She felt round, spongy, and bright. She had rediscovered her muse, and she was delighted as she marked her calendar for a new rendezvous with the professor!

Get the sequel, *Warm Intrigues*, and find out more about the lives of Tyre(Trey) and Phoenix. Here is a sneak peek!

Chapter 1
The Rendezvous

"Yes, we will meet somewhere in the middle," said Phoenix. She and Trey (Tyre) had finally decided on a rendezvous after that chance and second meeting on Fifty-Seventh Street Beach. He would be coming from Evanston, and she would be coming from Homewood, Illinois.

When he called her at the appointed time, they agreed to meet at Leona's on Taylor Street because of its central location and quaint atmosphere. The ongoing music videos also served as a comforting backdrop during lively conversations. They almost said "Leona's" in unison as they talked about choosing a comfortable eatery in the heart of Chicago.

"Trey? Or should I say Tyre?" she asked again during his phone call.

"Call me Tyre, pronounced as 'tire,'" he answered. All she knew is that he was a widower in his thirties. She was one of the first people to whom he introduced himself by his given name and not his nickname, Trey. She was attracted to this college professor and was impressed by his intellect and good looks, but she would let him share the details of his life—only when he wanted and what he wanted.

He, in turn, had never met such a beautiful librarian when he initially met her at the Homewood Library. She was not only knowledgeable but also quite refined. He was used to librarians looking like the stereotypical ones, but not this one. They had not shared too much during that second meeting at the beach, but he knew that she was a woman who had experienced her share of pain.

He figured that a solo trip to the waterfront usually signaled that someone was in deep thought. He privately hoped that he would be around long enough to find out more about her. He figured most people in their thirties had had some knocks in life.

"Okay, I will be there at 1:00 p.m.," she said.

"Okay, see you there," he added and hung up the phone.

Phoenix started her Saturday morning with her normal routine of making coffee, reading her spiritual messages, and journaling until she felt she had amply given thanks for the last twenty-four hours of living. When she felt sustained and fortified for the day, she pulled out the clothes she would wear on her first date with Tyre.

She worked on her makeup after showering and had to pause to stop her racing heart. She reminded herself that she was almost as giddy as a schoolgirl. She slowed down to breathe. She went to sit in her easy chair, and she lightly touched the unusual rock that they had found on the beach that day. He offered it to her and told her that his given name, Tyre, had some connection to a rock. That was another story that had to be finished by this intriguing and handsome man.

Tyre answered the ringing phone as he emerged from the shower. "Trey?" boomed his father.

"This is Tyre here," he said, grinning. "I took your advice, and I will now go by my given name that will give me increase so I can stand like a rock."

"Yes, and stand as powerful as the tradesman of old stood on the isle of Tyre. They were known for the selling of purple dyes. Read up on it," his father said.

"Purple also means power," added Tyre.

"So glad you were listening, son. I just wanted to call to give you a dose of confidence as you move forward in your life. Good luck on your first date with—" He paused. "What's her name again?" asked Elisha.

"Phoenix, Dad. Her name is Phoenix. Phoenix Matthews." Tyre smiled as he talked.

His father was quiet on the other end of the line. He was giving a silent moment of thanks and gratitude to the Great One. His son was sounding like his boy again! There was a sigh of relief that life went on for his son after the carnage of his former wife, Flora.

"Dad, are you still there?" asked Tyre.

"Yes," Elisha said, coughing. "My coffee went down the wrong way," he lied. "Have a good time and enjoy yourself, son."

"Okay, Dad. I will call you in a few days," said Tyre. He hung up the phone.

Tyre, wrapped in a large towel, sat down in his favorite chair. He sat still for a moment before he ventured out to meet this beautiful and smart woman. Thoughts of her brought warm feelings. He picked up his daily meditation messages and gave at least twenty minutes to the routine to become focused before going to meet the world.

After the mishaps with his former wife, he was hopeful that he had the courage to establish a relationship with someone with whom he was equally yoked. He knew in his heart of hearts that a good connection would strengthen and not exhaust him. He hoped that this Phoenix could be the answer to his need for a good woman.

Bibliotherapy

Cohen, B. 1989. *Snow White Syndrome*. Jove.

Dickinson, E. 1976. *Complete Poems of Emily Dickinson*. Back Bay Books.

Dyer, W. 1976. *Your Erroneous Zones*. Avon.

Eddy, M. B. 1994. *Science and Health with Key to the Scriptures*. The First Church of Christ, Scientist.

Emerson, Ralph Waldo. 1993. *Self-Reliance and Other Essays*. Dover Publications.

Fillmore, C. 1978. *The Twelve Powers of Man*. Unity School of Christianity.

Gibran, K. 1964. *The Prophet*. Borzoi Books.

Goldsmith, J. 1962. *The Art of Meditation*. George Allen & Unwin.

Holy Bible, The. 1975. The National Bibles International.

Holmes, E. 1938. *The Science of Mind*. G. P. Putnam's Sons.

Kupferle, M. 1983. *God Will See You Through*. Unity School of Christianity.

Mandino, O. 1968. *The Greatest Salesman in the World*. Bantam Books.

Ponder, C. 1968. *The Prospering Power of Love*. Unity Books.

Russianoff, P. 1984. *Why Do I Think I Am Nothing Without a Man?* Bantam.

Shinn, F. S. 2009. *The Power of the Spoken Word*. Wilder Publications.